THE TRAIL TO RETALIATION

PLAINSMAN WESTERN SERIES BOOK TWO

B.N. RUNDELL

WOLFPACK
PUBLISHING
— EST 2013 —

The Trail to Retaliation
Print Edition
© Copyright 2021 B.N. Rundell

Wolfpack Publishing
5130 S. Fort Apache Rd. 215-380
Las Vegas, NV 89148

wolfpackpublishing.com

Paperback ISBN 978-1-63977-002-1
eBook ISBN 978-1-63977-003-8
LCCN 2021950207

THE TRAIL TO RETALIATION

Our future is bright with promise, yet there are always shadows of concern and question that try to rob us of that promise. I dedicate this book to those of you that are determined to let God provide you with a future and a promise, (Jeremiah 29:11), and are willing to go boldly into that future. Sometimes we need to sit back and listen, maybe read a little to relax, and I trust this book will give you a few moments of escape, and perhaps a challenge and encouragement to take on another day. God bless you, my friends.

G ranny's name did not suit her. Most would think of a Granny as a doddering old woman with grey hair, a cane, and reading spectacles hanging precariously on the end of her nose. But the Granny that owned and operated Granny's Boarding House was an early war widow who was at most in her mid-forties but looked younger without a touch of grey in her auburn hair, and nothing about her walk or ways fit the description of doddering. Rachel McAdams was the envy of the women of Kearny, the hopes of the single men, and the regret of the married men. Always one to be friendly with everyone but never over friendly with anyone, she was an excellent cook and a savvy businesswoman.

Reuben Grundy pushed back from the breakfast table that was crowded with ten other men and the school marm who would share teaching duties with Claire Beckham, the war widow who Reuben escorted out to Fort Kearny from her home in Iowa. Her farm had been hit and ransacked by a band of renegades calling them-selves the Home Guard, a band that was chased and

1

killed by Reuben who was on a bit of a vengeance run after they struck his family farm and killed his parents.

"Ma'am, I certainly thank you for another fine breakfast." He leaned back, patting his paunch and added, "I reckon I've gained more'n ten pounds this winter, and it's all because of your fine cookin'!"

"Well, I'm always glad to hear that my cooking is doing its job, proper," declared Rachel, smiling and nodding to Reuben as she refilled the coffee cups of her boarders.

"It is that, ma'am, it certainly is that. But if you'll excuse me?" he asked, nodding to the others at the table and standing. He turned away and started for the door, a busy day before him. The winter had been what the locals called an 'open winter' with very little snowfall, but plenty of cold weather. What moisture that did come was in the form of drizzling rain that froze when it hit the ground and made life miserable for animals and man alike. Reuben kept his blue roan horse at the local livery and whenever the weather was tolerable, he spent the days riding the countryside, oftentimes bagging game for the soldiers at Fort Kearny, or occasionally for the folks at the boarding house.

Although the war was still underway in the east, and there were rumblings south and east of Kearny, there had been little action, other than recruitment efforts, in the Nebraska territory. Reuben had done his duty when he volunteered early and served with Berdan's Sharpshooters and quickly got his fill of killing. But when he returned home to find his family farm burned, his parents murdered, and his younger brother killed by over-zealous soldiers, he had to fulfill a promise to his older brother, Rufus, who died in his arms in the military hospital, to take care of things at home. And to 'take care of things' set him on the trail of the murderous band of phony Home Guard to avenge the deaths of his family.

Now he was west of the war and glad of it. Always one with a generous helping of wanderlust in his character, he had longed to see the west and start a new life, but doing just what, he had yet to determine. He had considered a job offer with the Butterfield Stage Line to ride guard on the stages to the Colorado Goldfields, and a suggestion by Colonel Whitworth of Fort Kearny to ride herd on a wagon train that would head west in the spring, but he had yet to settle on a direction although he was considering just getting a pack horse and gear, loading up and pointing west and see what comes.

As he walked up the long street of the bustling Kearny, he watched the town coming alive with merchants sweeping the boardwalk, the lazy dogs lifting an eyebrow, chickens squawking down the alley ways. He went to the livery for his horse and to get the latest town news from the smithy, Guillame, or Gill, DeLaurentis, the big man with the French accent and the broadest smile in town. The big man was pushing open the massive front doors as Reuben walked with the rising sun warming his back and greeted his friend, "Mornin' Gill! Lookin' for a big day are ya?"

"No, mon ami. I like ze lazy days when I can sleep ze day away!" chuckled the big man, his rotund belly bouncing as he laughed and his accent coming and going as he wished. He turned to face Reuben, "Grab some o' that firewood and we'll get some coffee going!" motioning to the stack of wood that lay against the corral fence.

Reuben picked up an armload and walked through the big opening into the shaded interior, the morning sun doing its best to warm the front of the livery. The smithy was stirring the coals in his forge and reached for the coffee pot that always sat at the side of the fire, shook it, and walked to the water bucket to refill the pot. Reuben asked, "How many?"

"Ahh, there are twelve wagons so far, but I think there will be more soon." He looked up at the bluing sky, "It will be a good day today and some more will come. But," he began, pausing as he sat the coffee pot near the forge, added the firewood for the fire, then turned back to Reuben who stood leaning against one of the posts that held harness and more, "four men came from the east," nodding to three horses in the nearby stalls, "said they were taking a wagon train west."

Reuben frowned, detecting more in Gill's tone than his words, "But..." prompted Reuben, stepping closer.

"But, zay do not look like wagon train guides. Maybe soldiers running away, maybe brigands, but not guides."

"You don't say," mused Reuben, walking to the stalls, looking at the horses and the tack stacked nearby.

"Oui. I do say. If I was going west, and they were going west, I would go east," declared the smithy, nodding, and reaching for his meerschaum pipe. He busied himself stuffing the tobacco in the bowl, glancing up at Reuben. He had come to know Reuben over the past few months as they waited out the winter and knew him to be a man dead set against those that would do wrong by others. Although Reuben was not a lawman, the smithy had learned about the deeds of Reuben, not from Reuben himself, but from those he helped along the way, the new pastor of the church, the Carpenter and Walters family, and the young widow woman, Claire Beckham, all very generous of their praise for the young man.

"Where are they stayin'?"

"Ze hotel, of course," laughed the smithy, for the 'hotel' as it was called was little more than a false front hiding a big tent with bunks. Although the front end served as an eating place with long tables and benches to accommodate the soldiers from the fort that always wanted a change from the fare at the fort.

Reuben sat down near the big door, opposite the smithy, as the two men savored the stillness of the morning, the warm sunlight on their shoulders and the promise of a good day. Gill looked at his friend, "I always thought you would take the wagons west," as he took a long sip of his steaming brew.

Reuben frowned. "Me? I've never been west of here, how could I guide anyone?"

"You never came here before, but you found your way. Your friends tell me you even used the stars to guide you, is it not the same to go further?"

Reuben shook his head, "I never figgered on bein' responsible for anyone but my own self, and sometimes that's more'n I bargained for," he mulled, leaning his elbows on his knees, savoring the rising steam from the coffee in his hands.

"But I have seen you speaking to just about anyone that has traveled to the west and how you learn everything about every trail, river, mountain and more. I watch as you lock those things away in your mind, as if you were drawing a map in your head. You probably know more about the west than many that have been there, and you are a good man, the kind of man that always finds the right way to go and to help others. That is what these people," nodding toward the wagons parked behind his livery, "need more than those who would do them wrong."

"You really think they'd do wrong by the people? How so?"

"There have been many stories of wagon trains led into Indian territory and being massacred, others that were left in the mountains by leaders that took their money and left them to die in the snows of the mountains. Some that just got lost." He took another sip of coffee, looking over the rim at Reuben. "Have you not heard of the Donner party?"

Reuben frowned. "No, I guess I haven't."

"During the gold rush days to California, they were trapped in the mountains by the snow, turned to cannibalism to survive, more than half of their number died in the mountains."

Reuben shook his head at the horror of people resorting to such measures, but he also knew that when it came to the choice of survive or not, man was capable of many despicable acts. He shrugged, tossed aside the dregs of the coffee, and rose to replace the cup on the hook above the pot. He looked back at Gill. "Reckon I'll let Blue stretch his legs a mite. A good day for it!" he declared, looking at the cloudless blue sky. He walked back to Blue's stall, grinning as the big roan turned to look over the stall divider and greet his friend with a nicker and a nod of his head. The two had become inseparable friends, seemingly capable of reading one another's minds, and anticipating the moves and wants of each other.

Whenever Reuben left town, he was prepared for most anything, always carrying both his Sharps rifle and Henry rifle in the scabbards on the saddle, his Remington Army revolver in the holster at his left hip, butt forward, and his Bowie knife in the sheath at the small of his back. His saddle bags carried the military furnished binoculars, the telescopic sight for the Sharps, jerky, ammunition, and a few miscellaneous necessary items for traveling in the unknown. He was a confident, but well-prepared man, having learned much in his stint in the Army. Yet now, glad to be free of the war, he just wanted to wander, preferably alone.

The front blade sight settled into the notch of the rear sight, both centered on the low chest of the whitetail buck as he bent to drink of the water of the Platte. As the buck lifted his head and turned to face the thicket of sycamore where Reuben leaned against a big tree, the Henry rifle bucked and spat smoke and lead. The buck started to turn away, but the bullet found its mark and the animal staggered, stumbled, and fell. Reuben waited a moment as he jacked another cartridge into the chamber of the rifle, watching the deer for any movement, but it lay still.

With a slight nod and a grin of satisfaction, Reuben stepped from beside the tree and walked to the carcass, rifle held across his chest, always at the ready. But the deer was dead, and Reuben leaned the rifle on the rump of the carcass as he slipped his Bowie knife from its sheath at the small of his back to begin field dressing the prize. The blue roan was tethered in the trees and as soon as the deer was dressed out, Reuben walked to the woods to bring the horse near and drape the carcass over the rump of Blue. He stroked the roan's neck, scratched his head, and slipped the tether free, slid the Henry back in its scabbard as he turned back toward the deer, only to see three more deer tiptoeing to water's edge, less than a hundred yards downstream.

Reuben dropped Blue's reins to ground tie his friend, snatched the Henry from the scabbard and moved about ten yards away from the horse, dropped to one knee and took aim. Another shot, another kill. It took but a few moments for him to drape the buck's carcass over the rump of the roan, and a short while to dress out the smaller buck and hang it over the saddle. With two deer to carry, Reuben knew he would be walking, at least to the fort, to deliver the larger of the deer, but would ride back into town to take the second buck to the boarding house.

"If you ain't a sight fer sore eyes!" declared Sergeant Riley, master cook for Fort Kearny. "I thought I was gonna hafta give them sojers a double helpin' o' beans, and they wouldn't be too happy wit' me fer that, ya' darn tootin'!" The cook stepped close to help Reuben unload the buck from the rump of his roan. "This'ns a nice 'un! Got him some nice fat, I see!" nodding to the rim of fat that showed along the long cut where Reuben had gutted the animal.

"Well, I thought about gettin' close and pokin' around his ribs to make sure he was fat 'nuff, but they get a little skittish when you go pokin' 'em like that!" responded Reuben, enjoying his usual repartee with the cook. The short rations in the winter had given Reuben the opportunity and excuse to do more hunting and the soldiers appreciated the meat that seemed in short supply.

"Any sign of buffler yet?" asked the sergeant.

"Nothin' that I could see, but with the weather warmin', they'll prob'ly be along anytime now, I reckon."

"Hope so. One o' them wooly buggers last a bit longer'n these skinny whitetail. Taste better, too!" he declared as they hung the carcass from the overhead hooks. The sergeant would get a couple of helpers to skin and cut up the deer and the meat would probably be in the skillets before noon.

Reuben chuckled. "Enjoy!" he declared, tossing a careless wave over his shoulder as he turned back to Blue. "Gotta go see the colonel," he called as he swung aboard.

"Better you than me!" retorted the grinning cook, wiping his hands on his already soiled apron.

The commandant's office was in his home that stood across the compound from the mess hall and soldier's barracks, the entry facing to the east, shaded by a piazza along its entire front. Standing two stories high, the second story also showed a piazza across the entire front. Reuben tethered the roan at the hitch rail that stood sentinel before the veranda of the wooden building. He mounted the steps and pushed open the door to be greeted by a corporal seated at a desk in the outer office. The man looked up at Reuben, recognition showing as he nodded and grinned. "What'cha need, Reuben?"

"Like to see the colonel, if he's not too busy."

"Let me check," answered the corporal, rising to go to the door, knock and enter. He quickly returned and motioned Reuben to enter.

"Good morning, Reuben. I take it you've brought some meat for the mess hall?" asked Colonel Whitworth, motioning for Reuben to be seated.

"Yessir, but that's not why I'm here." He seated

himself and began, "There've been several wagons that have stopped in Kearny, many bound for the west, and there's been talk about organizin' a train. But I know your orders are no wagon trains less than fifty wagons are to leave here, and from what I can gather, there's some men in town sayin' they're puttin' together a train to leave right soon, and there's nowhere near fifty wagons."

The colonel breathed deep, pulling a letter from atop a stack of papers at the corner of his desk, glancing at it as he held it out before him. "I know something about that. Three men stopped in yesterday with this letter from Lieutenant Colonel John Pattee." He paused, looked up at Reuben who shrugged, not recognizing the name. "It seems that Pattee will be with Colonel Summers of the Seventh Iowa Cavalry, and will be replacing me in command of the fort. Now, normally, I would give little attention to something like this, but Pattee is the governor's brother-in-law." He looked over his spectacles at Reuben, watching the young man's reaction to the news. "This letter gives those men the right to form a company of wagons, and leave whenever they see fit, regardless the number. Now, what I know about Summers and Pattee, is neither of 'em have seen combat nor any battle with Indians. But, if I were a betting man, I'd say they will see plenty of action if they leave here with less than fifty wagons."

"There's nothin' you can do?" asked Reuben.

"Nothing. I'll be leaving as soon as I am relieved, which could be any day now. But, if there's anything you can do, go along with 'em, shadow 'em, what have you, that would be good. I understand you have a little experience with some brigands and have handled things with

11

ease, and you have an excellent record with Berdan's Sharpshooters."

Reuben frowned, surprised the colonel had any knowledge of what had transpired in the past year and more after he was discharged from service with the Union forces. He grinned at the thought. "But I had expected to put all that behind me and just head west myself, but I am concerned for the safety of families in the wagons. The smithy in town said he met the men that visited you and he wasn't too impressed with them, at least not in a good way."

"Nor was I, and if I were traveling west with my family, I wouldn't put my life in their hands, but some folks are more concerned about getting there, wherever there may be, before someone else, whether it's the gold-fields or farmland."

The colonel stood, pulled out the lap drawer of his desk and handed Reuben a shiny Liberty Head double eagle twenty-dollar gold coin. "By my account, that should square us, does it not?"

"Yessir. With the buck I just delivered to cooky, that makes ten at two dollars each. We're square."

Reuben stood, pocketing the coin, and extended his hand to shake. "And, Colonel, I wish you the best as you return to the east. Ohio, isn't it?"

"Cleveland is my home, and I will return there for a month or so, but then it's on to the war. Not certain yet what that will be, but..." He shrugged, forcing a grin as he shook Reuben's hand. "And may God go with you."

"Thank you, Colonel, and you as well."

WITH A PASSING GLANCE AT DOBYTOWN, JUST WEST OF THE fort, the notorious settlement that catered to the soldiers, always doing whatever was necessary to separate the soldiers from their meager pay, Reuben pointed the roan to the landing for the ferry to make his way across the Platte to Kearny and the boarding house. He hung the deer from the cross post on the back porch, promising to return and help with the butchering, and left to take Blue back to the livery.

"Howdy, Gill!" declared Reuben as he reined up at the front door of the livery. He frowned as he peered into the dimly lit interior to see the big smithy busy at his forge.

"Mon ami! It is good to see you!" he answered, motioning to the coffee pot that sat nearby.

"Gonna put Blue up first!" responded Reuben, letting the roan drink at the trough near the door. He led the roan to his stall, stripped the gear, and began rubbing him down with a brush kept at the stall. He quickly finished and put grain in the bin, then walked to the forge to pour himself a cup of coffee. As he filled his cup, he motioned to the smithy who was making the anvil sing with his hammer on a horseshoe and poured another for the big man.

When Gill finished, he dipped the shoe in the water, let it sizzle, and hung it on the overhead rack. He dropped the tongs at the edge of the forge and walked to where Reuben had taken a chair near the front door, accepted the coffee and seated himself opposite the young man. He sipped the hot brew, looking at Reuben over the edge of the cup, and asked, "What is it you want to know, mon ami?"

"You learn anythin' more about those three that are puttin' the company of wagons together?"

Gill shook his head. "No, they have not returned, but I did hear they're saying zey will leave soon no matter the number of wagons."

Reuben nodded. "Seems they have special permission from the new commandant comin' to the fort, some fella name of Pattee, brother-in-law to the governor of Iowa."

"Even with the Cheyenne, Arapaho, and Sioux doing what they do?" asked the smithy, frowning in disbelief.

"Reckon they either think they can handle 'em, or they think they can get past 'em, or..." shrugged Reuben. "Whatever they're thinkin', I don't like it." He sipped his coffee, looked up at Gill. "What do they look like?"

"Why?"

"Thought I might look 'em over, that's all. You can tell a lot by a man when you pay attention, and he doesn't know it."

Gill slowly nodded his head and began to describe the three. "Ze leader, big man, tall as you, broad shoulders, brown hair, clean shaven, ze women would call him han'som, but he has shifty eyes, will not look at'chu. Second man, my size, black bushy beard, long hair, tackety boots, beady eyes, and stinks. Other man, tall, skinny, hatchet face, white hair, white skin, scraggly beard, white but stained with tobacco, rotten teeth. Other man, shorter but solid," he spread his shoulders and flexed his muscles to explain, "thick hair and whiskers, brown, bushy eyebrows, I theenk he is a Mexican."

"They even sound mean, the way you describe them," chuckled Reuben, finishing his coffee.

"You stay away from them. One will hold you; others will knife you. They have knives at their belts and in their boots!" cautioned Gill.

"Well, I don't wanna confront 'em, just look 'em over. But if they up an' leave, or if they have any company, let me know about it, alright?"

"Oui, mon ami. You know I will."

Reuben stood, tossed the dregs of the coffee aside, handed Greg the cup. "I hafta go skin a deer for Granny!" and chuckled as he walked away.

A glance to the table in the corner showed Reuben the four men the smithy spoke about, but he went to the end of the counter and mounted a stool, showing no interest in the other men. It was the midday crowd that began to fill the restaurant with hungry men and a few women, and the noise of conversation, shouted orders, and the clang and clatter of pots, pans and dishes filled the place and crowded out any possibility of eavesdropping on the group. Reuben ordered the special of the day and coffee and took advantage of his line of sight from the end of the counter and facing the four men. The leader of the group, the clean-shaven man, was speaking animatedly to the others, often scowling at one or the other, emphasizing his words with a fist on the table that made the dishes dance. The others cowed, and dropped their eyes to their plates, nodding and listening to the man. Reuben tried to make out what was being said but his lipreading woefully lacked, but the manner of the leader and the others told Reuben much about the four, and he was immediately concerned about any families that might decide to join the bunch.

He finished his meal, downed the coffee, and rose to leave, giving a casual glance to the group in the corner, determined to brand their images in his mind. He pushed open the door, stepped aside for two women that preceded two men, probably their husbands, into the restaurant. Reuben tipped his hat to the ladies, nodded to the men, and stepped outside on the covered board-walk. He turned toward the boarding house, but a flutter of paper caught his attention and he turned toward the community bulletin board to see a printed flyer pinned hastily on the board. *Wagon Train Forming, bound for Oregon and points west. Meeting tonight in the church for all interested in learning about the new Homestead Act and in the early departure of the first train of the year.* It was signed, *Major William Pendergrast.*

Reuben shook his head, thinking of the colonel at the fort and his warning about the restless Cheyenne, Arapaho, and Sioux. He knew many of the families going west were fleeing the war, some admitted to being copperheads, those that were anti-slavery, but also opposed to the war. Some were seeking land for farms, but others were anxious to get to the goldfields in California and Colorado, the gold rush to Colorado more recent and promising. He could not fault men wanting to make a better life for themselves and their families, but to endanger those same families, unnecessarily, was wrong in Reuben's thinking. He had never been in a fight with the Indians, but he had spoken to many of the soldiers and frontiersmen that had experience with the different bands, and he knew that beyond Fort Kearny, there was little protection against any element, Indian or white man, that would seek harm on others.

———

"LISTEN," SNARLED OTIS, LOOKING AROUND THE TABLE AT the three other men, "the major's done right by us so far, hasn't he?"

Grumbles and nods came from the others as Otis continued, "Then we'll do as he says, at least till we collect our share. And what he doesn't know, all the better."

"What'chu mean, what he doesn't know?" growled the big man, Anton Pawlak, who the others called, 'Bull'.

"We've got a shipment coming of 'special cargo' I arranged for Kicking Bear, one of the new breed of Lakota Sioux. He and some of his cousins and friends, Flying Hawk, Black Fox and others are none too happy with all the 'white topped wagons' coming into their land and all the 'blue coat' soldiers. So, if they can keep some o' the soldiers busy out west, they won't be fighting our friends from the south. And it just so happens, with all that fighting going on, it makes perfect sense that a friend of mine at Jefferson Barracks in St. Louis, would be ordering all those rifles and such. Course, if some of 'em go missing, he just has to order more."

"But what about us an' the wagons? They gonna fight against us?" grumbled the tall, skinny one known as Griffin, but more often called 'Bugs'.

"No, no. They won't even get the goods till we're almost outta their territory, and they know that if they want more, well, they gotta keep us alive to do that."

"Yeah, yeah, I see," mumbled Bugs, his lack of what most would call 'smarts' evident.

"And I need you all at the meeting at the church tonight. And try to clean up a little. We want these folks to trust us, and we need to look, well, better'n you do now." He glanced around the circle of men. "It wouldn't hurt you to take a bath, Bull. Just being downwind of you ruins my appetite!"

"Ain't takin' no bath! I had one last spring when I crossed the river. Any more'n that ain't good fer ya," growled the big man, puffing up his chest and snarling at Otis.

"Then, maybe you better not come to the meeting."

"Good! Got better things to do anyhow!"

OTIS YEAGER SAT BESIDE MAJOR WILLIAM PENDERGRAST as they watched the crowd file into the church and find seats on the benches. Yeager leaned over, "Looks like we got us a good crowd. How many wagons you think we'll need to make up a train?"

"At least fifteen. That'll give you 'bout twenty men that can fight if need be, an' some of the women too. That should be enough to get you through Sioux country. They're the only ones making war talk now."

The men were speaking in low tones as they watched the couples entering the church. The major often nodding and smiling as he caught the eye of someone familiar, but his expression changed when Otis asked, "What about the Cheyenne? I hear their dog soldiers are making a few raids down on the trail."

"Nuthin' to worry about. I've made arrangements with Black Kettle; he wants peace and he'll keep his people away from any wagon trains."

"Yeah, well, the soldier boys were talking about peace with the Sioux and look what happened with Little Crow's War north of here. That was just last year!"

"You're sounding like an old lady! You scared of the Indians?"

"No, I just know enough about 'em to know they can

change their mind about as often as a woman changes her clothes!"

"You just make sure you get these settlers to Fort Laramie. Your job is finished but not until then," stated the major, standing to address the crowd. He rapped his knuckles on the pulpit to get everyone's attention and began, "Welcome everyone! Welcome. I'm Major William Pendergrast, and I represent the New West Land company. Now the reason I'm here, is to explain a little about the Homestead Act of 1862, and to tell you about some beautiful land that is there for the taking! Every one of you can file on 160 acres and build yourself a home that will be yours for generations!" He continued to speak about the requirements of the Act, how each family would have to reside there for five years, make improvements, and file the necessary paperwork, but went on to assure everyone that the New West land company was there to assist and ensure that everyone would be successful on their new homeland, even promising that his company stood ready to buy back any property that failed to meet their expectations.

"Buy back? But I thought the land was free for the taking?" asked a sandy haired man that sat next to a young woman who appeared to be in the early stages of pregnancy.

"Oh, it is, it is. But, after you've made improvements, maybe building a home and such, you will be investing your time and money, and we are there to help, if needed," answered the major.

"But why would you do that?" asked a colored man from the back of the room.

"Because we anticipate putting in a town in the same area. A town with a church, businesses, a bank, and more. We want the town to succeed as well and for that to happen, you must succeed."

The answer seemed to satisfy everyone and the major continued, "Now, if there are no other questions, Otis Yeager," motioning to the man seated beside him, "will be the captain of the wagon train that is forming. He and his men have made several trips over the Platte River Road, also known as the Oregon Trail, and they will be leading the train west. We'll be signing folks up following this meeting."

"But what if we don't want to settle where you're talkin' about? What if we want to go on to Oregon or Californy?" asked another of the prospective wagon men.

"This train will go to Fort Laramie, the furthermost military fort on the frontier. If anyone wants to go further, there will be other trains going through that you can join up with at any time."

That seemed to satisfy almost everyone, and the building was soon full of excited conversations, introductions between couples, and folks lining up to sign the roster for the train. Reuben had been sitting quietly at the back of the church, watching the goings on, and rose to leave, but was stopped by a man that sat nearby when he asked, "Excuse me, suh. Are you goin' to be signin' up to go on the train?"

Reuben let a slow grin split his face as he looked at the colored man, his wife holding tight to his elbow as he stood. "No, no. I'm not a family man and I won't be travelin' with the train."

"Well, suh. If you don't mind my askin', what'd you think of what the major said?"

Reuben sighed heavily, turning to face the questioner, and with a glance at the man's wife, he said, "I don't rightly know. I've always been one to do things on my own and don't like havin' to depend on what another man tells me, especially when that man has somethin' to gain. But, if you're lookin' to make a new life out west, get some free land, there are not a lot of other choices. But if you do choose to go, be sure to go well armed. There's a lot of Indian country you have to go through, and you'll need to bag some game for meat. Just," he paused a moment, looking from one to the other, "be careful of who you trust and always keep your weapons loaded and close by."

"Yes, suh! And thank you, suh!"

Reuben nodded, tipped his hat to the woman, and turned to leave. When he stepped into the darkness at the front of the church, he lifted his eyes to the stars, shook his head and breathed deep of the cool night air. He had the premonition of something unseemly on the horizon, but he was determined to see his way into the west. He was hopeful that his long-held dream was soon to be realized.

I t was early, Reuben had just left the boarding house and was heading for the livery, and to see a big Conestoga wagon rumbling down the main street was unusual, especially at this time of morning. The businesses were just starting to open their doors, and the sun was beginning to paint the eastern sky with its brilliant colors, and for a wagon to come through town at this hour would mean they either traveled all night or had camped just outside of town. While most travelers shunned the use of the big Conestoga wagons as too heavy and cumbersome, preferring the Studebaker wagon, or converted farm wagons of the type often referred to as Prairie Schooners. But this one was pulled by a six-up of mules and was loaded heavy, the creak and groan of the big wagon, and the squeal of the hubs on the axles told of the heavy load. Although the mules labored at their task, they showed no sign of lather or weariness, so Reuben guessed they had been camped near town and came in this morning, perhaps to join the wagon train that the major was gathering.

Reuben walked up the boardwalk trailing behind the

wagon and saw the big rig pull up in front of the livery and the man step down. Reuben paid little attention to the man, noticing the depth of the tracks of the wheels, the recent spring rain had moistened the soil somewhat and a wagon with a typical load of supplies and home goods would show its passing, but these tracks were deeper. *I'd like to get a look in that wagon, see what he's haulin' that's so heavy,* thought Reuben as he walked around the big rig and stepped through the door of the livery. He heard the smithy talking to the man but walked on to the stall with his roan.

"If you could take a look at it, I'd sure appreciate it!" declared the man from the wagon. He was standing beside Gill who was busy stoking up the fire on the forge. "Might just need some greasin' but I wanna make sure 'fore we head out. I understand there's a train leavin' soon an' I wanna be with 'em."

"I'll take a look see, just gimme a minute or two," answered the smithy, giving the man a sidelong glance with another toward the wagon that blocked the big doorway. The smithy wiped his hands, grabbed the spare tongue, and went to the wagon. Fashioning a lever and fulcrum, he hoisted the front axle off the ground by the problem wheel, blocked it up and started to examine the wheel. He looked up at the man, "Looks to be your hub, prob'ly needs some new metal on it. Take me a couple hours, cost you five dollars!"

"Do it!" declared the man, who glanced back at the woman who had climbed down from the wagon without his help and now stood, hands on hips glaring at the man. They started to leave until the smithy hollered, "Hey! Take care o' these mules! Less'n you want me to and it'll cost you another five dollars!"

The man looked at Gill. "You do it!" and looked at the

woman, waved her to move ahead of him and followed her around the wagon to the end of the boardwalk, stepped up beside her and motioned to the Blue Moon restaurant, saying something that could not be over-heard, but received a less than pleasant response.

The smithy shook his head, mumbling to himself as Reuben came close. "It's people like him that make me glad I deal with animals 'stead o' his kind!" as he started to the mules.

Reuben chuckled. "Well, to say the least, they don't look like a happy married couple. She looks like she fell off a bar stool, and he looks like he wanted to find one he could climb up on! Sure makes a fella wonder what they're takin' west in that big rig," nodding to the wagon.

Gill looked to the street, saw the two going into the restaurant and turned to Reuben, "Go 'head, take a look!"

Reuben looked down the street, glanced at the wagon and climbed up the tail gate, leaning into the wagon. He reached in and flipped aside a blanket to see several wooden boxes at the bottom of the wagon box. "Hah!" he shouted. He replaced the blanket and stepped down. He walked to the side where the smithy was wiggling the wheel off the hub. "Several big boxes, couple marked 'Farm Tools' and one marked 'Bibles', but they're the same size and look to be the same."

"Maybe they're Beecher's Bibles," suggested Gill, frowning at Reuben. "You know what that is don't you?" But a frown from Reuben gave his answer. Gill contin-ued, "It was a term used before the war by Henry Beecher, a preacher that thought the Sharps rifle would be more effective fighting slavery than the Bible and shipped the rifles by marking the boxes as 'Bibles'."

Reuben frowned. "Never thought of that," he responded, looking around for a tool. He spotted a pry bar, picked it up and climbed back into the wagon. The squeal of loosened nails came from inside as he lifted the edge of the lid of the crate marked 'Bibles'. He shook his head as he looked at a full crate of oil paper wrapped rifles. He pulled one up to get a better look, recognized the type and replaced the weapon, the lid, and the blanket. With a quick glance around, he jumped from the wagon, and handed Gill the bar. "Springfield rifles."

"What'chu suppose they're gonna do with them?" asked Gill.

"Dunno, but I reckon there's 'bout a hundred rifles and ammunition in there. Maybe more," he reached for the coffee pot, shook it, pursed his lips at Gill. "Want some?"

"You need to ask?" responded the grinning smithy, as he rolled the big wheel aside. He began taking measurements of the hub and the surrounding metal and began removing the worn and twisted metal. He would use the old as a pattern for the new, but he would need to make some modifications. As he pulled off the old metal, he glanced up at Reuben. "Think they might be for the Indians?"

"Or maybe some Southern sympathizers. Can't imagine those are just for settlers out west. But maybe if he's outfittin' a tradin' post or somethin' like that."

He sat down, sipped his coffee, looked up at Gill. "You ready to sell me that mule?"

"You leaving?"

"Ummhmm. Figgered today or tomorrow. I'll need the packsaddle and panniers too."

Gill looked at his friend, sighed heavily. "For you, mon ami, thirty dollars!"

"Everything?"

Gill nodded, sipped his coffee, looking at Reuben

over the rim of the cup. "But you have to help me put that wheel back on!" pointing with his chin to the wheel leaning against the post.

"Deal! Do I have time to go to the emporium to get my supplies?"

"Oui, oui. This will take an hour or so, maybe less."

Reuben rose and tossed aside the dregs, replaced the cup, and started toward town. As he stepped up on the boardwalk, he saw the man with the wagon and his woman come from the restaurant and stop on the boardwalk to talk to the one who called himself Captain Yeager. It was obvious they were not strangers, especially when the woman tiptoed to kiss the captain on the cheek. Reuben crossed the street to the emporium, showing no recognition of the group, stepping up on the boardwalk and entering the storefront.

He handed his previously prepared list to the storekeeper and offered, "If you can tally it up, I'll pay you and let you get it ready then come back later for it."

"That would be a big help. I'll fill it, but you won't need to pay till you pick it up, that way if you think of anything else, we can just add it to the tally."

"Good, good. I need to ready the animals and packs, then I'll stop by later," replied Reuben.

He returned to the livery, saddled the roan, and waited until Gill was ready to replace the wheel. Within a few moments, the big man finished with the hub of the axle, nodded to Reuben and to the wheel which Reuben rolled close to the hub. Gill finished greasing the hub, added some to the inside hub of the wheel, and both men lifted the big wheel to slide it on. Satisfied, the smithy replaced the nut and lowered the wagon with the lever and fulcrum. He looked at Reuben as he stood wiping his hands, frowning. "You going somewhere?"

"Ummhmm. Thought I'd talk to the colonel about those 'Bibles'."

Gill grinned. "But you're leaving?"

"Ummhmm. That makes it the colonel's problem and not mine."

"Sounds reasonable, but I think you will still be, how you say, involved?"

"I hope not, but we'll see," answered Reuben, knowing he could not just let the men with the wagon train, who obviously were up to no good, get away with endangering the lives of so many families. But he shook his head as he rode from the livery, thinking, *all those men are older than me, family men, most of 'em, and should be able to take care of themselves.* But the words of his father came back, "You can't let evil run rampant. If you can do something to stop it, then you've got it to do. You can't leave it up to others."

"Yeah, but if the colonel and his soldiers can take care of it, then..." he realized he was speaking aloud and looked around to see if there was anyone near that heard him, but he had already moved away from the town and was approaching the ferry to cross over the Platte to the fort. He chuckled to himself, reached down and stroked the neck of the roan. "I know you heard me, Blue, but you understand, don't you?"

"And that's about it, Colonel. But I thought you should know about it," stated Reuben, sitting across the desk from the fort's commandant, Colonel Whitworth.

"I appreciate you telling me about it, Reuben, but with the train leaving soon, and my replacement coming any day, I'm not sure what we can do about it. I will tell my replacement, but I can't send any men with the train, we only do that when asked and if the size of the train warrants the protection."

"Seems the small trains need more protection," offered Reuben.

"You're right, but with Pattee's name on that letter given me by the organizers, that kind of ties my hands."

Reuben sighed heavily, rose to his feet, reaching across the desk to shake the colonel's hand. "Well, Colonel, I wish you the best."

The colonel also stood, accepted Reuben's hand and replied, "And to you as well, Reuben. Maybe after the war we'll cross paths again."

"I'd like that, Colonel. But until then, Godspeed."

H e rode into the setting sun, golden lances piercing the last of the darkening blue sky, clouds blushed with orange and pink hues, the horizon fading into a dark shadow. He had taken the time to say goodbye to the friends that made the journey from the east last fall, the Carpenters, Walters, Claire and little Charlie, and Parson Page. The parson encouraged Reuben to continue with his Bible reading, giving him a gift of a leather-bound Bible. His parting words were, "Remember, Reuben, sin will keep you from this book, or this Book will help keep you from sin."

"I wish it were that easy, Parson, but it seems everywhere I go there's somebody needin' help and that help usually ends up with somebody else dyin'."

"Just remember, Reuben, God used David to slay Goliath to save his people, Israel, and sometimes He may put you in the place of David, as He did last fall. Don't ever regret being used by the Lord to save the lives of others."

He hoped he might find some peace in the wilderness of the west, if there was any wilderness left. He had talked with many men that had been west, some old timers that had spent their early years trapping beaver, others that had lived in the mountains, some with Indians, and ended up scouting for the army or wagon trains full of settlers. He was surprised to learn that more than 300,000 people had crossed the Oregon trail en route to California or Oregon territory. He could not imagine so many people, yet the trail was hard packed from the passing of so many wagons.

He lifted his shoulders, sucking deep of the cool evening air, smiling at the fading colors of the sunset. He enjoyed this time of day, the beginning of night. Although it often brought memories of his time with the Sharpshooters when he had to stalk the men in grey and take them down in the first light of morning. But there was a stillness in the darkness that could not be found at any other time of day, the quiet, a softness under the blanket of night. Even the night sounds were lighter, mellow, soothing. It was a time when he could ride in the moonlight, and reminded him of the times he and his father would take a skiff out on the lake at night and move so slowly as to leave few ripples in their passing. That was how he felt sitting astraddle of Blue, the horse that had become one with him and seemed to enjoy the stillness with the only sound the soft plodding of his hooves and those of the pack mule that followed, the whisper of their passing through the fresh green grasses of springtime.

Reuben glanced back at the mule, who trailed a bit to the side, choosing his own path and coming with a slack lead, his head high, ears pricked and eyes wide, searching the shadows. He was pleased with the way both Blue and the mule, Jack, had buddied up. The smithy had put them in the last two stalls in the livery, giving them time to get acquainted with one another, and now they seemed to wade through the grass to the same cadence. He planned to stay near the trail, but take his own path, giving him opportunity to observe the wagon train that was set to leave come morning. Traveling by night would keep him well ahead of the train, and free to keep watch as they followed, although he was hopeful there would be nothing of concern. But that old nagging feeling kept crawling up his backbone and settling in his gut that had often been the harbinger of something bad, and he could not shake the feeling.

The moon was waxing full and hung high in the eastern sky, bending its shafts of light over Reuben's shoulder as he made his way along the trail. He would stay the course to put some miles behind him, then take his own path, probably between the trail and the river where the tall growth of hardwoods and others would provide ample cover for his camps.

The thin line of grey at his back prompted Reuben to start looking for a campsite. The river made a slight dog-leg bend to the northwest and a bend like that usually offered grassy flats. He was near the ragged tree line on the south side of the Platte, big cottonwoods stood above the wide spreading bur oak, sycamore, and elm, and the undergrowth of service berry, choke cherry and willows hid the river from sight, but the chuckle of the wide shallow river sang a lullaby to the tired rider, and he pushed his way into the thickets. A clearing of low growing willows and grass was inviting enough for him to rein up and step down. He quickly stripped the animals of their gear, let them roll in the grass and have a good drink, then rubbed them down and tethered them nearby.

Within a few moments he had a small fire going,

using only the dry broken branches that would make an almost smokeless fire, but with added caution he placed the fire under the wide overhanging branches of the big oak, knowing the budding leaves on long branches would dissipate any smoke. He sat the small coffee pot on a flat rock, having filled it with water from a small but clear feeder creek that came from western flats. With biscuits from the boarding house, willingly offered by Granny Rachel, and some warmed-over bacon, he was satisfied with his meal and went to his blankets just as the eastern sky blushed pink and red. With a last check of Blue and Jack, he pillowed his head on the saddle seat, covered his eyes with his floppy felt hat, and was soon sound asleep, trusting the animals to stand watch.

HE FELT THEM BEFORE HE HEARD THEM, GIVING HIM childhood thoughts of his father shaking him awake, but the clatter of horns, bellow of bulls and anxious cows, and the musky smell told Reuben it was not his father, but a massive herd of buffalo making its migratory trek north. He had expected to see buffalo, just not so soon, and not so many. He walked to the edge of the trees and saw the brown blanket that stretched west and south into the distance beyond his eyesight.

A heavy cloud of dust rose above them, and the constant rumble of hooves, horns, and bellows sounded like a basso profundo chorus in harmony with the other, now muted, sounds of nature. He grinned at the sight, marveling at the vast herd that seemed to stretch endlessly in all directions. He chuckled at the antics of the calves romping beside their mothers, their orange coats contrasting with the deep brown of the herd. Cowbirds rode atop many of the beasts, pecking away at their feast of ticks and bugs, tolerated by the bison because of their complementary attentions.

The herd seemed to slow, and several dropped their heads, snatching at any grass that was still standing. Bulls moved to the side, finding dry wallows to roll in and coat themselves with dust to protect their thick furs. The big dust cloud began to settle, and the herd stopped, spreading out across the grassy flat, the bulls dragging their beards across the tall grasses, snatching at anything within reach.

The blue roan nudged Reuben with his nose, making him turn to see riders on the far side of the river. Looked to be about a dozen natives, but Reuben was not well acquainted with the tribes, yet there was something familiar about the group. He remembered a time last fall when he was traveling with the wagons and had encountered a bison herd migrating south, and a band of Pawnee confronted him as he sat watching and anticipating some fresh buffalo steak. He looked at the warrior at the head of the band and nodded as a slow grin split his face. He recognized Big Spotted Horse, of the Pitahawirata band of the Pawnee people, the leader of the band of hunters he met last fall. It had been a friendly meeting where Reuben took several buffalo for the natives and conversely was befriended by the band when they visited the camp of the wagons and taught the women much about preserving the meat and more.

He had not been seen by the Indians who were intent on the herd, and he drew back in the trees, Blue beside him. He kept his eyes on the hunters, watching and waiting yet noticing there were several that were armed with rifles, more than before, and these rifles were Springfields. Frowning, Reuben wondered if these rifles came from the men that were joining the wagon train, for it was not that common for even friendly natives to be armed with such weapons.

He slipped the Henry from the scabbard as he watched from the trees, his eyes constantly roving and searching the far bank as well as the near side for any other threats, but there were none. Reuben had no need to take a buffalo, as he was amply supplied for his journey and one buffalo would feed at least two families for most of a month and would be too much for him to pack on the already burdened mule.

Big Spotted Horse dispersed his hunters, motioning and sending them to different points of the grassy flats and once satisfied, he gave the agreed upon signal and the hunt began. Rifle fire thundered and the entire herd moved as one, not in a panic or stampede, but a slight jump, startled by the sound. But these, the largest animal of the plains, had few enemies other than man and were seldom frightened into a stampede. Yet the continued barrage, the screams of riders charging into the fringes of the herd, drove the herd into a moving mass of brown, driven and led by boss bulls and herd cows. The bellowing rose as a thunderous rumble, the pounding of millions of hooves into the soft soil of the grassy plains, the rattle of horns clashed with the racketing of rifle fire and screams of charging warriors.

Reuben leaned against the pale smooth trunk of a tall sycamore, feeling the rumble of the herd vibrating even the towering trees. A quick glance showed new growth leaves fluttering as if blown in a breeze, but the wind was still, only the earth moved and breathed with the rumble of thousands of buffalos moving as one. It was past midday when the last of the herd followed the trampled and churned earthen trail and river crossing, leaving behind the carcasses of the kills. Reuben breathed as if he had been in the chase, the excitement waning as he watched the hunters gathering by the carcasses for the ritual of eating the steaming liver dipped in bile.

He had not watched the far side of the river until he saw the caravan of women and horses trailing travois coming for the butchering of the kills. He turned away, checked the tethers of his animals, and returned to his blankets, believing himself to be out-of-sight of the busy hunters and the women as they worked. He was at least two hundred yards from the nearest kill and the cover was thick and Blue was ever watchful as Reuben stretched out, rifle at his side, pistol in the holster, hat over his eyes. He had developed the habit of getting sleep whenever he had the opportunity, knowing there would soon come times that rest would be elusive and even more appreciated. He closed his eyes and was soon asleep, hopeful of that undisturbed and much needed rest.

I f it were possible to sleep with one eye open, that would have been an apt description of the habit of Reuben. Although he had confidence in Blue to keep watch, he had learned long ago to sleep light or wake up dead and he preferred the former. It was full daylight, the Pawnee had been hard at work butchering their buffalo kills, and Reuben was trying to crowd in a few hours of sleep before he took to the trail under the waxing moon.

The deep chested rumble that came from Blue brought him full awake, but only his eyes moved, scanning the clearing before him. He slept with his back to a heavy thicket of underbrush with dried leaves, thin brittle branches and a few thorns that gave protection from any that would try to move through the brush, but the clearing was wide open, and he saw the long shadow slowly nearing. His Remington Army .44 was in his hand, thumb on the hammer and finger alongside the trigger. He breathed lightly, watching the shadow and the sudden move of a raised arm caused him to throw aside the blanket, roll to his back and lift the pistol. He dropped the hammer as he saw the uplifted warclub about to descend. The pistol roared, bucked, and spat lead, fire, and death, striking the charging warrior, and stifling the scream of his war cry. The conical bullet caught the warrior at the base of his throat, blasting out the top of his backbone and neck, splattering the brush and grass with blood and detritus, his body falling in a heap at Reuben's feet.

Reuben came to his feet, earing back the hammer on his pistol as he moved in a crouch, searching the trees and brush for another attacker. He moved toward the stack of gear, bent to slip the Henry from the scabbard and holstered his pistol. He jacked a round into the chamber of the rifle, continuing his search, knowing the shot would bring others of the Pawnee into the trees. He sidestepped away from the animals, moving beside a big sycamore and with a quick glance to his rear, he turned back to watch the tree line at the big meadow's edge.

They were spread out as they entered the trees, following the slight path he used when he entered the clearing and probably the same way his attacker came, but they moved wide into the trees and Reuben counted four warriors approaching. A familiar figure stepped from the trees, rifle in hand, as he looked from the tethered animals to the stack of gear, to the dead warrior crumpled at the foot of the blankets.

"Big Spotted Horse," called Reuben, showing only the muzzle of his rifle beside the pale trunk of the tree. "I am a friend; we have hunted together. This man attacked me when he thought I was asleep, and I had no choice but to shoot."

The three warriors broke out in war cries and screams, demanding vengeance on the killer of their fellow warrior, but they were stilled by the uplifted hand of Big Spotted Horse.

"Who speaks from hiding and says he is a friend?" asked the big leader of the Pawnee.

"I am Reuben, the man with the far-shooting rifle, who killed buffalo with you last fall."

The big man lifted his head and let a grin tug at his mouth. "You are a friend. Come," he motioned for Reuben to come into the clearing.

Reuben kept his rifle at the ready as he moved from the trees, watching the angry warriors to either side of the leader and walked toward Big Spotted Horse. As he came close, he extended his opened hand to shake with the leader of the Pawnee and the man accepted and shook Reuben's hand enthusiastically. He looked at the dead man, shaking his head, "Black Badger was like his name, always looking for trouble." He turned away, motioned to the others to get the body, and waved for Reuben to walk beside him. "Badger was anxious to get a rifle and we were waiting for some traders to bring more rifles to my people. They said they would come with many rifles as they did before, but they have not come."

"I thought the traders were not supposed to trade rifles with the Pawnee?"

"It was that way, but many of our people have been asked to serve as scouts with the soldiers and we were told we could have the same rifles as the blue legs."

"Were these soldiers that traded you the rifles?"

"No, no. A big man, hairy face, smells bad, he is called 'Bull', and another man, face and hair like snow, skinny, 'Bugs'," explained Big Spotted Horse.

Reuben nodded his head, knowing exactly who Horse was talking about, but he chose not to say anything, not knowing what the plans of the men were, but suspecting they were not planning on meeting with the Pawnee, maybe waiting until they were further from the Fort and make a more profitable trade with other tribes that were not as friendly as the Pawnee.

"You will eat with us," stated Big Spotted Horse, motioning to the fire where several women were gathered. "We will eat and return to our village. Are you going west alone?"

"Yeah, I'm travelin' alone and plan on goin' so far west there won't be any people!"

"I remember when I was young," holding his hand at his side to show the height of a youth, "and there were few people in this land. But then the white wagons came, and the land is full of people. Now the white eyes fight each other, much like the native peoples have done. I think there will never be a time again when there are no people unless we all kill each other."

As Horse spoke, Reuben listened closely but also noticed the woman of Big Spotted Horse and another, younger, that kept glancing his way showing a coy smile whenever he caught her eye. When Horse paused, Reuben responded, "I pray that it doesn't come to that, my friend, for there is much country I have yet to see and many people I have yet to meet. That is why I left the war in the east to the politicians and professional soldiers and came west, to get away from all that."

They sat apart from the cookfire, enjoying the fresh buffalo steaks and more. The women tending to their needs, adding meat to their platters, drinks to the gourds, and the young woman continually hovered close to Reuben. They talked of many things, hunting, fighting, families, and friends. When they finished the meal, the women were already busy packing things for their journey, bundling meat in the hides of the buffalo and loading it onto the travois. Big Spotted Horse had noticed the glances of the woman and Reuben and smiled knowingly as he began to explain. "She," nodding to the young woman, "is Running Fox, the sister of my woman. Her father had promised her to Black Badger, but she did not want to be with him. Badger was determined to make her his woman, other men were afraid of Badger and would not try to gain her favors. But now, she is pleased she is no longer to be given to the man who has been killed. She smiles at you and if you would like, she will warm your blankets for you and go with you."

Reuben's eyes flared with surprise and a touch of fear. "Uh, uh, hold on! I'm not lookin' for a woman. I got places to go and things to do, I don't need a woman."

Big Spotted Horse rocked back on his elbows, laughing, and choking on his drink, until Reuben stood and looked from Horse to Running Fox and back to Horse. "You need to tell her to take her pick of the men of your village, but as for me, I'm packin' up and leavin'. Now!"

The men walked to edge of the trees, chuckling and Reuben shaking his head, glancing back at the women. They said their goodbyes and Reuben watched as Big Spotted Horse returned to his camp, mounted his horse, and started the cavalcade back to their village, his woman, and her sister beside him. Running Fox turned to look at Reuben, smiled and waved as she slapped legs to her horse to hurry to the side of another warrior.

Reuben watched the band file out of the big meadow, taking the same river crossing used by the herd of bison and disappearing past the band of trees that lined the river. He turned back to the clearing and began rigging the horses, smiling at the thought of Running Fox, which added motivation to his wanting to put a few miles behind him before dark when he would stop for another rest and meal. The wagon train would be at least another day behind him, and he wanted to thoroughly scout the trail and area before they came near, and he looked forward to some time in the saddle, the best place for thinking, to consider what he should do about the gun peddlers and leaders of the train.

A LONELY MAN, REUBEN HAD ALWAYS KEPT TO HIMSELF, enjoying his own company more than that of others. When need be, he could talk with others, even make friends, but somehow, he always retreated into himself, pondering his ways and the ways of others. He was used to the wilds for he was a hunter, taught by his father who gave what he called *wilderness lessons* to Reuben and his brothers, lessons that included the many ways and tricks of fighting. It had become a common practice for the three boys to go into the woods and have a knock down drag out fight to see who would emerge with fewer marks or wounds and yet be 'top dog' of the woods.

But it was more than just the how-to of fighting, it was the why of it. His father often sat them down in some lonely clearing, maybe with a cane pole and string in the creek and taught. He often extolled the beauties and handiwork of God yet reminded them it was a land to be tamed and made safe for others, families with women and children. And for a land to be safe, there had to be law and order and if that were lacking, it needed honest men to build the country into what he believed the Creator intended. "There's too many that just want to take what they want, walk over whoever stands in the way, and plunder the land. It takes real men to stand up to that kind, to educate themselves and learn to build something worth having and passing on the next generation, and I believe my sons are that kind of men!" And just the memory of those words made Reuben sit tall in the saddle, knowing he was the last of the family and he had big boots to fill.

The sun had tucked itself away, leaving behind the fading colors of sunset as dusk settled across the flats. The crossing of the bison was well behind him, and Reuben pointed Blue to the northwest, following the often-deep wagon ruts of the trail. The river chuckled off his right shoulder, hidden behind the thick foliage of spring greening of the trees and shrubbery. Tall grasses were stretching up from the warm soil eager to find the warmth of the day's sun but would only find the cooling breeze of the evening. Now nearing knee high on the long-legged blue roan, the gramma, bluestem, and buffalo grasses would soon be tall enough to tickle the bellies of both the roan and mule.

With the last light of day laying low across the plains, the grasses moved with the breeze like the waves of the ocean, heads laying down as if to rest, fresh green stems catching the light as the white capped waves of the prairie. Reuben sucked in the cool air, filling his lungs with the freshness of freedom, and basking in the fading light and the coming night, foretold by the early stars that could linger in obscurity no longer, sending their arrows of brilliance to announce the coming star filled canopy of darkness and silence.

With a gentle nudge, Reuben turned Blue to the edge of the trees to search out an alcove in the greenery for a short rest and maybe some hot coffee. But Blue resisted, pausing to look to the northeast and some gathering clouds and back to his rider, and pointing with his nose to the coming storm as if to say, "Find shelter 'fore that gets here," then pushed on toward the tree line.

"Maybe you're right, Blue. Might be best to find some cover or make us a shelter to sit it out. Don't look too promising, does it?" He reached down to stroke the big blue's neck and peer into the thickets before him.

The grassy clearing was ample and near enough to the water with several tall sycamore and maple standing away from the riverbank while a cluster of cottonwoods preferred the moister soil. Reuben stepped down with a wary eye to the clouds, and quickly stripped the gear from the animals. With axe in hand, he went to work to make shelters for them all. He cut several skinny cottonwood saplings and lay the longer two between the branches of two cottonwoods, the next between the one cottonwood and a close by sycamore. Using long strips of sapling bark, he tied the cross pieces to the branches, and went to the thicket of maple and cut an armload of saplings. He formed a lean-to between the cottonwoods, using the maple saplings for cover, crisscrossing them for strength and laying the extra branches atop. For his own lean-to, he used the remaining saplings and branches, overlaying them with his rubber Gutta-percha ground cover and more branches.

With thick grasses underneath, his blankets stretched out with the gear under cover, he was ready for the storm, but chose to use the intervening time to make

some supper and coffee. His small Dutch oven was sufficient for his recipe of buffalo stew with meat from the
Pawnee, timpsila gathered on the trail, and his own
fixings of dumplings. With one eye on the hanging pot,
the other on the approaching storm, and an occasional
glance to the dancing coffee pot, his appetite increased
with the wind. When it appeared that the storm was
soon to be upon them, he grabbed pot, coffeepot, and
cup, and headed for his lean-to. As he sat with his back
to the cover, his face toward the fire, the wind whistled
through the branches high above his head.

The trees began to move, bending with the force of
the gale, whipping their branches like skeletal arms
shaking off the curse of the long winter. The whistle
slowly changed to a low howl, then the eerie sounds of
ghouls and phantoms began to tell their tales of coming
woes as the distant thunder beat the cadence of darkness
to which the storm marched onward. The sudden blast
of lightning startled Reuben, loosing an exclamation of
shock that brought an answering snort and blow from
Blue. "It's alright boy, just skeered me a mite," responded
Reuben, reassuring the animals he was close.

The stabs of lightning flashed and crashed in the
darkness as the rain came splattering about, knocking
fresh growth leaves from their tenuous holds on the thin
boughs. The blast of thunder and the following echo
rolled across the plains, marching ever onward before
the downpour. But the lean-tos were sound and shed the
water and the rhythmic drumming of the big raindrops
began to lull them all to sleep. The warmth of blankets
was inviting, and Reuben folded them back, but was
stopped by the dampened shout from the trees, "Hello
the camp! Can I come in!"

Surprised, Reuben hesitated but a moment, and

shouted his answer, "Come on if you're friendly! But know I've got a rifle aimed at your belly!"

The splashing and crashing of a man leading his horse was barely heard above the storm, but the man came close to the waterlogged fire. "I saw your fire, been tryin' to make it. Got room fer another'n in there?"

"Put your horse with the others an' come on," replied Reuben, scooting to the side nearest the big cottonwood and the horses. He kept his eye on the man, getting a brief glimpse of a waterlogged and buckskin attired weathered face in the flash of lightning. As the man ducked under cover, he looked at Reuben, offered his hand, "I'm Jim Bridger, sure glad to meet'chu!"

Reuben leaned back for a better look at the man, shook his head at the drowned rat looking figure and answered, "I'm Reuben."

"Well, Reuben, I be thankin' ye, yessir. This storm looks like it'd pick a man up and carry him away, if you was to let it!" He looked around, sniffing. "Is that coffee I smell?"

"Ummhmm, there's some left," answered Reuben, nodding to the pot that sat at the edge of his blankets. He had been eating from the Dutch oven and offered Bridger, "Want some stew?"

"Stew? I never turn down food, no sir. Just pour some of it on that lid, I'll use it fer a plate. Got muh knife right'chere an' it'll do me."

Reuben chuckled as he poured out a good portion of the stew into the rimmed lid of the Dutch oven and handed it to the visitor. A broad smile split his weathered face and he pushed the hair from his eyes and forehead, nodded his thanks, and started eating. "Ummm, buffler! They already comin' north?" he mumbled around mouthfuls.

"Yup," answered Reuben, finishing his portion before the man asked for more. He cleaned out the pot and set it aside, looked at his visitor and asked, "Which way you headin'?" knowing that to ask a man too much was looked down upon in this part of the country, for many had a past they wanted to forget.

"East! Goin' to Fort Kearny, meetin' up with Colonel Whitworth."

"If he's still there," replied Reuben, leaning back on his elbow, looking at his visitor in the dim light offered by the occasional flash of lightning.

"What'chu mean, still there?"

"He's bein' replaced. Gettin' sent back east to join the war. Some politician's hand-picked replacement comin' to take over," explained Reuben.

"What 'bout them wagon trains and the Injuns?"

"Well, Whitworth didn't want any less than fifty wagons to a train, but the new rules don't say that. Matter of fact, there's a train of about fifteen wagons not too far behind me."

Bridger shook his head, drawing his feet up close as he sat spread legged. "Not good, uhuh, not good. There's a young Sioux buck name'a Kickin' Bear that's got big ideas and he's got a good bunch o' followers that's joinin' up with him. Flying Hawk, Black Fox, and plenty of others are showin' their intents by stirrin' up war talk. Not a good time to be goin' through this part o' the country."

"Were you a scout or sumpin'?" asked Reuben, frowning as he looked at the man who sat scowling and shaking his head.

"Uh, sumpin', I guess. I scouted for some sojer boys that went out to Fort Laramie. Ran into some Cheyenne, Arapaho, but the worst was them Sioux!"

They took to their blankets to wait out the storm and get a little shuteye before the coming of the dawn. Although the storm lessened, it continued its drizzle until the early morning hours and gave way to a star-studded night that displayed its lanterns as if there had never been a cloud in the sky. As the sun began to herald its coming, the men rolled from their blankets and joined forces to find some firewood which resulted in them breaking off lower branches from the cotton-woods, some of the heavy bark and feathery under bark, but they soon had a fire going and coffee perking.

Reuben mixed up some biscuits and sat the Dutch oven on the coals at the side of the fire, scooped up some more with a piece of bark and loaded the lid. He sat back and looked at his visitor, who appeared to be a man up in years, Reuben guessed him to be late fifties, early sixties, both being old for a man coming from the mountains. He wore a flat brimmed felt hat over his beady piercing eyes, rumpled sun-bleached brown hair, a square jaw and a brimming confidence that could only come from experience. He had a glint of mischief in his eyes, and crooked grin that lifted one corner of his mouth, and wore a fringed buckskin jacket and buckskin breeches.

"Been in the mountains long?" asked Reuben, stirring the fire with a long stick.

"First came to the mountains in '22 with Ashley's brigade. Been roamin' 'em ever since."

"This is my first time, anxious to see the big Rockies."

"Ain't nuthin' like 'em," began Bridger, a glaze coming over his eyes as he lifted one hand as if he were touching the mountain peaks, "they's so big, looks like they're the pillars of the sky. Those tall peaks, some holdin' snow year-round, just stick their granite heads up and look down on all of the Good Lord's creation and smile." He paused, basking in the memories, "When you first see 'em, you think they're right out there," nodding to the distant flats, "but three days, mebbe a week later, they's still out o' reach. And when you get close, you feel like you cain't hardly breathe." He chuckled. "'Course the closer you get, the higher up you are and the air do get a little thin, makes it hard to breathe. A flatlander like you, you get up on them mountains, take three, four steps, and you hafta stop and suck air." He chuckled again at the memory.

Reuben breathed deep, his shoulders lifting as he poked the fire with the stick, and with a glance to Bridger. "Trap beaver?"

"Done that quite a spell, but the market died an' had to do other things. Scoutin' for the army, other expeditions. Couple years back I took the Raynolds expedition west, was gonna go to the land of many waters, that's what the Shoshone call the land where there's lots of geysers an' such, but the early snow kept us from goin' that far north. We crossed over a pass I found, called it Union Pass, dropped into Green River country, where we had some ronny vous' back in the year.

"Then I hooked up with the army, guided some sojer boys to Fort Laramie, and now I'm headin' to Fort Kearny. Gotta tell them about the tribes that are gettin' restless with all the settlers comin' into their country." He shook his head. "Onliest thing keepin' 'em from a big fight is they ain't got white man's rifles. If they was to ever..." He shook his head as he accepted a cup of coffee from Reuben, troubled by the thought of armed Indians declaring war on the settlers in the wagon trains.

"Uh, there's somethin' you need to know," began Reuben as he started to tell Bridger about the rifles he discovered in the wagon at Kearny. "I told the colonel about it, but since he was bein' replaced, he chose to leave it to the next man. But," Reuben squirmed a little as he poured his own coffee, "the letter he got about the men gettin' the wagons together was signed by the new commandant and his assistant, a well-connected lieutenant colonel."

"You think they know about the rifles?" asked Bridger, frowning.

"I'm sure Colonel Whitworth told them, but the couple with the wagon claim to be startin' a tradin' post or somethin' like that, and the boxes are all marked 'Farm Tools' or 'Bibles'."

Bridger ground his teeth, his cheek muscles flexing as he tossed the dregs of the coffee aside and rose to his feet. "I'm gonna head to the fort, see if I can talk sense into them sojer boys. You keepin' an eye on that train?"

"I am."

"Then I might be back, mebbe with some sojers."

"The Pawnee are north, south and east of you, but you'll soon be comin' up to Arapaho country, it'll be south and west. Sioux country is north of the North Platte, so that's after the split in the rivers. This here's the land of the Kitkehaki Pawnee, prob'ly the bloodiest o' the bunch! They take scalps, whether it's from another tribe or white man, they ain't par'tikkler. They also make human sacrifices, usually a captive girl, so's to have good crops an' such. So, keep careful watch, an' like you was thinkin', travelin' at night's not a bad idee." Bridger stepped into his stirrup and swung aboard his bay gelding, that looked to be about the same age as his rider. He reined the horse around, looked back over his shoulder to Reuben. "I'm gonna try to be back an' help you wit' them gunrunners, but..." A shrug finished his sentence and he waved over his shoulder as he dug heels to his mount.

Reuben watched as Bridger kept to the trees, and soon disappeared behind a cluster of sycamore. He turned back to his mounts, standing hip shot, waiting patiently for him, and swung aboard his blue roan and pointed him just west of north, bound for the low hills beyond the flats. The word of caution from Bridger had prompted him to ride to the hills where he would have a better promontory to look over the country and better cover in the event of unfriendly company.

While Bridger rode into the rising sun, Reuben felt the warmth on his back and right shoulder. The roan was feeling frisky after the night's rain and stepped lively through the wet grasses across the flatlands, and as usual, the mule followed close behind, off to the side, the slack in the lead showing his eagerness to keep pace with the roan. They passed an island of trees and shrubs, most blooming. Reuben recognized Redbud with the rosy, pink flowers opening wide to the sun, refreshed after the night's rain. Another tree was showing some greenish-yellow buds that he thought might be a Buckeye, and as they rode past the thicket, he got a whiff of some wild plum and service-berry with their white blossoms waving in the morning breeze.

He angled his path a little to the north, looking back across the grassy plains to the distant river, now about three miles away. The hills were shouldered together off to the left, none rising more than a couple hundred feet above the valley floor, but they would offer him enough of a rise for a good view of many miles of the wagon trail, and the surrounding countryside. Bridger had said the Kitkehaki Pawnee were more of a threat than the Arapaho, but that could always change depending on the mood of the chief or war leader of the band. And the Pawnee would be on the far side of the river, but the Arapaho would come over the hills behind him. As he thought of the threat of the Natives, he could not help but take a long look along the face and flanks of the hills on his left, wondering if there was a war party watching him as he rode.

With another glance across the flats and to the river, he angled closer to the hills, always watching for an escape route and cover in case of a random attack. He thought on the words of Bridger, "What'chu always gotta remember, you're a white man, and to the Indian, you're rich with things that would make him all-fired important among his people. You've got a couple fine rifles, a pistol, and I saw a Bowie knife at'chur back. And that ain't even countin' what'chu got in them packs there. So, friendly or not, a native sees what'chu got and that makes you fair game. They set some store by a warrior that can capture or kill a white man and take all his goods. Even to sneak up on you and steal what'chu got, that's big medicine to a warrior lookin' for honors!"

As he considered the counsel, he thought on the goods he was carrying. Half of the load on the pack mule was trade goods, awls, knives, pins, needles, verdigris, vermillion, small mirrors, combs, buttons, blue and white beads and several axes and metal tomahawks. Hopefully, those goods would help him make friends with the Native people, maybe learn from them the ways of the wilderness.

He turned up a low draw, heard the trickle of water and found a good spot for his midday break and rest for his animals. He guessed he had come about twelve or more miles and the animals had slowed their pace a mite, telling him they wanted to rest. With a couple scraggly cottonwoods for shade, a freshwater stream, probably spring fed, and good cover in the wide gulley, he resolved to rest the animals and enjoy some coffee before he climbed the butte beside the draw for a good look around the territory.

He bellied down atop the butte, stretching out with his binoculars as he overlooked the flatlands before him. The river was a little over two miles away, easily seen by the trees that sided the stream, and the grassy flats seemed to weave side to side, giving way to the mild breezes that pushed through the wide plains. To the north, the plains were shouldered by the lower rolling sandy hills, and the dry land hills on the south. Where he was positioned, atop a round butte that was freckled by juniper and cedar, he had a good view on this clear day for several miles in all directions.

He watched a herd of pronghorn antelope grazing in the grass just below the hills to his left and well away from the river. A bunch of white tail deer were high stepping their way to the river, grazing on the fresh green grasses as they moved. Back to his right, he spotted a reticulated white snake he recognized as the wagon train, but they were too far back to count the wagons or to see the outriders. He glanced at the sun, back to the train, and thought they would probably come about even with his previous night's camp, maybe even further north and closer to his overlook. That would give him the opportunity for a close-up look at the train and the riders, but he would do so covertly, preferring the men of the train to remain ignorant of his presence.

He walked back down the butte, digging in his heels where the slope was steepest, and was greeted by a nicker from Blue and a glance from Jack. They were enjoying the graze beside the little stream, and Reuben decided to roll out his blankets for a snooze, hoping to catch-up on his sleep from the stormy night and his visitor. He chuckled at the thought, remembering the few times his plans of sleep actually materialized, and wondered just what would disturb him this time.

But fortunately, he was able to get a good nap and stretched awake with the cold muzzle of Blue on his neck. He reached up and stroked the roan's neck and face, talking to him as he stood up and looked around. The mule was grazing contentedly, and nothing seemed amiss, so with a glance to the sun, he grabbed his binoculars and mounted the butte once again. It was late afternoon, the sun at his back, and the wagons had made good progress. Less than two miles away, they appeared to be continuing on and would probably be pretty near his camp before they circled up and made their own camp.

He made a survey of the land around them, looking for any sign of Pawnee or Arapaho, but saw only the antelope herd and some deer. Across the river and in the flats beyond, he saw the wide swath of churned soil that marked the passing of the big herd of bison, but there was no sign of any other life than the wagon train. He was relieved at that, and crabbed back from the crest of the butte, sat up and started down the hill.

He had no sooner returned to camp, than the mule brought up his head, ears pricked as he looked down the draw, watching a bunch of deer picking their way deeper into the hills. Reuben slipped the Henry from the scabbard, stepped behind the cottonwoods, and waited. When the lead buck neared, he looked at each animal, saw two does with fawns at their sides, another doe, a pair of yearlings, a young button buck, and a larger buck whose antlers were just showing. He narrowed his sights on the button buck, waited until he was in a clear line of sight, and slowly squeezed off his shot.

The Henry blasted, pushed against Reuben, and sent the .44 slug on its way. Reuben had taken a small sight, focusing on the neck just behind the head and the slug flew true. The buck winced, his head tossed to the side, stumbled, and fell forward, kicked once, and lay still. At the blast, the other deer jumped and took off as a group, bouncing through the low shrubs and disappearing in an instant. Reuben waited a moment, watching the buck and satisfied, stepped from the trees, and walked to the carcass. He poked the ribs but there was no movement, and he leaned the rifle against a rock, went to one knee as he withdrew his Bowie knife and began the work of dressing out the deer.

He knew he would either smoke the meat, make pemmican, or lose much of it to waste, but with the wagons near, he thought he might find someone that could use some meat and he would share, maybe keeping some back straps for himself. Within a short while, he had the deer cleaned, skinned, and divided out as to what he would keep and what he would share. He split the hide, lay a front quarter and hind quarter on each side, put the back straps atop his panniers, and began his clean-up.

He glanced to the lowering sun, knew dusk would soon lower its curtain, and he readied the two packs of meat to load on the pack saddle on the mule to take to the wagons, but that would wait until after full dark. First, he wanted to look them over and that would require another climb up the butte.

T he moon was waning from full, now about three quarters, but the sky was littered with several small clouds that blotted out much of the star lit sky when Reuben gathered up the lead of the pack mule, leaving Blue tethered in his camp and started for the wagons. The train had circled up at the edge of the trees and he noted the big Conestoga had its tailgate facing the tree line, making him wonder about their intentions.

He moved along the base of the hills until well below the wagons before crossing the slightly rolling plains. Choosing a low swale for cover, he led Jack across the flats and into the woods beside the Platte. Picking his way carefully through the trees, moving as stealthily as possible, he had no reason to be concerned about the mule for they were by nature soft-footed, always choosing each step before moving.

A glance at the stars showed it to be nearing midnight, but there were still fires burning within the circle, making shadows and silhouettes of those that sat about. Leaving Jack in the trees, Reuben silently moved closer to the wagons, always watchful for any guards or wandering men that might sound an alarm. A fire near the Conestoga showed several shadowy figures, the light allowing Reuben to recognize the big man, Bull, and the white-haired albino called Bugs. Three others had their backs to Reuben, and he guessed them to be rest of the bunch that headed up the wagons.

"I don't care what the major says, we done alright when we made the deal with the Pawnee. I say we sell 'em what we got and hightail it outta this country!" growled the big man, glaring at the others.

"You sold one case and you didn't get but what, five hundred dollars? That's nothin' compared to what we can get from the Sioux! We got eight cases of Spring-fields, and that'll get us eight thousand dollars!" responded one of the men with his back to the wagon. Reuben suspected him to be the one they called 'Captain'.

"Is that after the major takes his share?" whined the white-haired man, appearing afraid to look directly at the others.

"No, but he said it's ours to split among us," answered the captain.

The men looked to one another, grumbling, and complaining until Bull said, "How soon till we get to Sioux country?"

"Why you asking me? You've been this way before. Sioux country is north of the fork of the rivers, so that's what, three more days?"

"Then we can go our own way?" asked the smaller man whose back was to Reuben, making him the one called the Mex, or 'Zeke'.

"Maybe, depends on how the Indians pay us. S'posed to be in gold coin, seems they raided a couple o' paymasters bound for Fort Laramie."

"Good! Then I can take my pick o' the women when I

head outta here!" growled Bull, eyes flashing in the firelight.

"You leave the women alone! We can sell the rifles, take the money and run and no one'll be the wiser, but if you take a woman with you, every man on this train and a whole troop of soldiers'll be on your tail!"

"Dunno, that Betts woman's been lookin' me over and I think she wants to leave her ol' man behind, and that girl o' hers," his big middle bounced as he laughed and cackled like a crazy man thinking about the women.

"I'm warnin' you, Bull, ain't no woman worth two thousand dollars! Especially when it's my money!" declared the captain, shaking his finger at the big man.

But Bull was not cowed and growled, "I'll do what I want, when I want. And I'm thinkin' I want that woman with yeller hair!"

Reuben moved back in the trees, looking at the rest of the wagons. It appeared most of the families had turned in for the night and the other fires were fading. He saw a man snuffing out a small fire, then stand with a hand at his back as he looked around. It was the colored man he saw at the meeting for the wagon train. Reuben smiled in the darkness, glancing back at Jack and the packs of meat. He looked at the man again, saw another man walk near and speak to him, then walk on to his wagon just beyond that of the coloreds.

Reuben bided his time, watching and listening as the men by the fire turned into their blankets nearby, some under the big wagon. He looked over the entire train, saw no movement, which meant there were no guards. He shook his head at the failure of the wagon master, knowing they were in Pawnee country, but all tribes raided in the lands of their enemies and this land was no exception.

He went to the mule, lifted one of the bundles to his shoulder, and started toward the wagon past that of the coloreds. Reuben had perfected his stealth when he and his brothers stalked game in the woods and now moved as silent as the night breeze. He hefted the bundle onto the tongue of the wagon and returned for the second bundle. Within moments he was beside the wagon of the colored man, but movement beneath the wagon made him slowly drop to one knee. He watched the shadow beneath the wagon, recognized it as the man in his blankets, mumbling in his sleep as he rolled to his side. Reuben waited a few moments, unmoving, until the breathing of the man became regular, and his muffled snoring told of his deep sleep. Reuben rose, walked to the wagon, and carefully laid the bundle on the ground beside the man, then moved away.

THE SCATTERED CLOUDS HAD FADED TO SHOW THE lanterns of the night hovering high above. With the moon doing its best to light his way, Reuben rode below the shoulders of the buttes and hills southwest of the river, keeping the darkened hills behind him, the grasslands between him and the river, he was confident of his obscurity in the shadows of the night. With about four hours before daylight, Reuben wanted to increase his lead on the wagons, and now with the hills pushing the plains between them, the river finding its way along the bottom of the grassland, and the river splitting and forming a wide island between the two courses, the wagon trail was pushed closer to the hills and Reuben.

With another glance to the sky, he knew daylight was on its way and he turned up a draw between a pair of round top buttes, looking for a place to camp and await the wagons. He rounded the butte on his right, took a shallow draw behind it and found a sheltered area on the back side of the butte with a cluster of junipers, grass, and a trickle of water. Stepping down, he led the mule close in and began stripping the gear from both animals. In short order he had the gear stacked by the junipers, his bedroll stretched out beside the stack, and was gathering firewood for his breakfast.

WITH HIS BELLY FULL AND THE SUN BRINGING WARMTH TO the day, Reuben mounted the butte, binoculars in one hand, Henry rifle in the other. Once atop, he made his way to a cedar, made himself a seat in the shade of the gnarly tree and began his scan of the area. Directly opposite his promontory the two courses of the river caught the morning sunlight and bounced it off the ripples showing Reuben the nearest course was the wider and probably older of the two, yet further on, the winding course of the lesser stream showed new growth trees that stood apart and offered a good view of the grasslands below the rolling sandhills north and east of the river.

As he searched the terrain, he spotted the usual herd of antelope, a few deer, and just inside the tree line a black spot caught his attention. He focused in on the spot, recognized it as a mama black bear with a pair of playful cubs trailing behind. They soon disappeared in the trees and Reuben turned his attention downstream, looking for the white topped wagons. He thought he had made about seventeen or eighteen miles in the night and that would be a good day's travel for the train, but it would be a while before they neared his promontory, probably nearer dusk.

Movement caught his attention and he turned back to look beyond the far course of the river to see several mounted warriors, as near as he could judge, Pawnee. He counted eighteen, all warriors, and although hard to be certain from this distance, he thought they were wearing paint. As he watched, they crossed the lesser stream, coming up on the broad island between the courses. Although there were trees on the island, they were not as dense, nor as tall as those on this side of the river, probably due to the changing course of the main stream. The Indians dismounted, all but two who had been sent ahead and started across the wide Platte. Reuben kept his binoculars on the two riders, saw them duck into the trees, but soon came from the thickets and started down the wagon trail towards the coming wagons.

He turned the binoculars back to the island, saw the rest of the band scattering out, finding places in the shade to tether their horses and stretch out for some rest. He carefully scanned the band, looking for anything familiar, wondering if this was the band of Big Spotted Horse, remembering his remarks about the traders and the guns. But try as he might, he could not identify any of the warriors, they were just too far away. He settled down in the shade of the cedar, and with his crumpled hat on a flat rock for a pillow, he began to snooze, knowing the rising sun would soon be in his face and would wake him.

It was a little stream of sweat that rolled from his brow, across the bridge of his nose and down his cheek that brought him awake. He looked around, seeing nothing alarming and sat up, scooting closer in the shade and lifted the binoculars for a look see. Across the way, the Indians were mounting and starting for the water, but paused as the two scouts splashed across to report their findings. Reuben turned to see the white-topped snake coming into view near the trees that sided the river. *Now, if the train has outriders, scouts, or at least someone that knows what they're doing, they'll be circling up and getting ready. So, do I try to warn them? Even if I rode all out, I couldn't get there without bein' seen by the Pawnee.* He looked at the flats before him and back along the trail, judging distance and time. He was an experienced sharp-shooter and long-distance shots came naturally to him and his big Sharps, but...

"Bull, you do the scoutin', Bugs and Zeke, you ride flank," ordered the captain, pointing with his chin as he directed the men in their duties for the day. The sun was barely peeking over the low horizon, the colors had faded, and the pale blue washed the grey from the sky. As the three men rode away to their points, the captain hollered to the lead wagon, "Let's roll!" waving his arm overhead to get the wagons on the trail.

The Betts family wagon was in the lead, George, who was a butcher by trade, and Mabel, his blonde-haired wife, were on the spring seat and their daughter, thirteen-year-old Madeline hung over the tailgate, watching the other wagons fall in line for the day's travel. They had started midway in the line and each day the wagons rotated with the lead wagon going to the end of the line and the next one taking the lead. She watched their saddle horse tug at his lead, reluctant to follow, and spoke to him, "Aw, Paleface, don't fight it. You know it don't do no good." Although they had only the one horse, she claimed him as her own and had named him Paleface because the blaze between his eyes seemed to melt

65

around his nose giving him the look of one that dipped his face in a bucket of whitewash.

Maddy looked at the wagon following theirs, driven by Fredrick Hampton with his wife at his side, but she was more interested in the two boys, one riding on each side of the family wagon. The oldest, Asa, was fifteen and his brother, Abner, was thirteen. She waved at Asa who smiled and waved back, making her smile even more. She had been flirting with Asa and had been giving him a lot of thought, or daydreaming about him, but he had been reluctant to return her attentions. Abner was a little more enthusiastic and had often come to their wagon when the train stopped, usually with an excuse to help or just to talk with Maddy, but her interest was directed at the older brother, Asa.

This was the beginning of the fourth day on the trail and it usually took a week or more before most folks had the opportunity to get to know many of the others on the train, but young people are seldom hindered by social graces nor intimidated by strangers and are often more eager to meet new people. Although Maddy had talked with the Betts brothers, she had also met the twin girls of Hiram and Hannah Hightower. The girls, Dorcas and Dinah, were only nine, but were friendly and always happy. The other girls on the train were all younger than her, but Maddy was more interested in the boys anyway.

Although the spring grasses were showing green, and the trees and shrubs along the river were budded out and waving their leaves at the passersby, there were few flowers in bloom, although the serviceberry bushes were showing white, and a few small patches of violets and Golden Alexanders added a little variety to the fresh greens of Spring. The first few days had covered the wagons with a thin layer of dust, but the rainstorm had washed everything clean, and it was refreshing to be on the trail and not be blanketed with dust. The creak, groan, and rattle of the wagons mingled with the rattle of trace chains, the flapping of the canvas tops against the braces, and the crack of whips all lifted together in the chorus of the trail that had become a welcome harmony that spoke of dreams and hopes to be fulfilled.

THE SCOUT USUALLY RODE A MILE OR TWO AHEAD OF THE wagons, usually staying on the same trail, watching for any hazards or any Indians or highwaymen that might cause trouble. They also were expected to bag game and leave it hanging for those on the train to fetch as they passed by, but Bull was not too concerned about what the others had to eat and paid little attention to that part of his job. As the sun climbed to its zenith, he took to the trees for a little rest for both him and his horse and to make himself some coffee and maybe fix something to eat.

They were in Pawnee country and the Pawnee were known to be friendly with the settlers and wagon trains, so Bull was not concerned about any danger from them, although he had bargained with Big Spotted Horse about some rifles a while back and had failed to deliver on his promise. He shrugged as he thought about it, no sense selling rifles for twenty dollars, when the Sioux would pay fifty dollars. He grinned at the thought of having his share in his pocket and a woman, maybe that blonde Betts woman, on his arm. He would show her what a real man was, and she could learn to make him happy. He chuckled aloud as he thought of her and stirred the little fire under his coffeepot. But unknown to him, the two

Pawnee scouts watched from the sycamore thicket just yards away.

Bull heard something in the trees, and he quickly stepped away from the fire, moving beside a big oak, pistol in hand. "Hey, Bull! That yore coffee I'm smellin'," came a familiar voice from the trees. A black horse with a diamond blaze on his face and one white stocking on his front left leg stepped from the trees with a white faced, white haired man aboard.

Bull stepped from the tree, holstering his pistol. "Yeah, it's mine and I reckon you can have some, soon's it's ready. What'chu doin' over'chere? You s'posed to be ridin' flank, acrost the river!"

Bugs swung a leg over the rump of his horse, stepping to the ground and dropping the rein to ground tie the black within reach of the grass. He looked at Bull as he neared the fire, "Yeah, but I wanted to talk to you without the others around."

"What fer?"

"What we gonna do 'bout them Pawnee wantin' the other case of rifles you promised?"

"Nuthin', we'll be outta their territory sometime tomorrow an' we won't never see 'em again."

"Don't be so sure 'bout that. I cut sign of a good-sized party of Injuns back yonder. Looked to be follerin' the train an' that could be them Pawnee lookin' fer their rifles."

"Fresh sign?"

"No more'n a day old, mebbe even early this mornin'," answered Bugs, reaching for the coffeepot.

Bull huffed and snorted, stood and walked around the fire, kicking everything in reach and snapping sticks with his fingers. "That blasted Injun! You just cain't trust 'em! Make a deal with 'em and next thing ya know they be huntin' yore hide and wantin' yore scalp!"

"But, Bull, you're the one that didn't keep the deal!"

"That don't matter!" he roared, kicking at a half-buried stick that was an exposed root and he shouted, "Yeeow!" as he grabbed his foot, dancing on the other one. He dropped to the ground, holding his foot, and jerking off his boots. He tossed the boot aside and gently pulled down his holey sock to expose a bleeding and bruised big toe. He looked around, stood, and hopped on one foot to the river's edge and stuck his foot in the water, dropping to his haunches on the bank.

Bugs followed him to the river's edge, asked, "Need some help, do ya, Bull?"

"No!" barked the big man. "You get on back where you belong, keep your eye on the tracks o' them Pawnee, an' if'n they get too close or sumpin', you come a runnin'! Got that?"

"Got it!" answered Bugs, turning back to the fire for a quick refill of his cup, but the growling from Bull sent him to his horse instead and he quickly swung aboard and kicked the horse into the water to cross over and resume his job as flanker.

Bull struggled to replace his sock and boot, limped to the fire, and doused the flames with the remainder of the coffee. He put the pot in his haversack behind the saddle and mounted his bay gelding and nudged him back to the trail. But he rode wary; always watching the trees beside the river, thinking that if the Pawnee were coming after him, they would come from across the river and through the trees and if he were watchful, he should have time to get away and warn the wagons. Yet it was not the wagons that concerned him; it was being caught out in the open alone and having to face Big

Spotted Horse and his warriors, all of them angry and looking for rifles. He shook his head, twisting around in his saddle, looking everywhere, fearful of just about everything.

By mid-afternoon, Bull was beginning to relax, thinking the party seen by Bugs must have been someone else or if it were Big Spotted Horse, he was not looking for Bull. Yet he still watched and listened, and it was nothing he heard, but just that feeling when the hair on your neck stands tall and the creepies run down your spine. He reined up, standing in his stirrups to look ahead, slowly sat back in the saddle and as an afterthought twisted around in his seat. Directly behind him, well within bowshot, were four Pawnee warriors, painted for war. Each one held a Springfield rifle, probably the ones bought from Bull, as they sat glaring at Bull. He started to rein his mount around, but when he turned in his saddle, suddenly there were four more warriors on the trail before him. He started to lift his hand in a sign of peace, but he saw others coming from the trees, four more warriors riding abreast and coming directly toward him. He quickly thought of the hills to the south of the trail, and slowly turned to look that direction, but more warriors seemed to spring from the ground and stoically sat, watching the lone white man. Bull turned toward those in the trail before him, saw others riding up behind them and recognized Big Spotted Horse.

Bull forced a grin, stood in his stirrups and lifted his hand to look to the chief, "Big Spotted Horse! Greetings! I was lookin' for you!"

The chief was sided by two others, one with a buffalo horn headdress and a hair pipe bone breastplate, carrying a war club with buffalo horns polished to a sharp point and eagle feathers trailing below. Three scalps hung on the shaft of the war club. Bull tried to remember the man's name, but his mind was chasing other thoughts and he could not bring it to mind. Spotted Horse rode close, "Do you have our rifles?"

"Sure, sure. That's why I was lookin' for you. I got 'em in a wagon on the train that's followin' me. I can get 'em to you tonight! You got the money?"

"You did not bring the rifles as you said you would. Now you are leaving with our rifles. I do not believe you were looking for us. You never came when and where you agreed."

"No, no. That wasn't my fault. The rifles hadn't come till the train was ready to leave and I couldn't get 'em for you. But I can now, you can have 'em tonite! If you got my money, that is."

Spotted Horse slapped a leather pouch that hung at his belt, making the coins within rattle and eliciting a grin from Bull. "Good, good. Now here's what we'll do. After it gets good and dark, you come to the trees, there'll be a big wagon, bigger'n the others, backed up to the trees and..."

He continued to explain his plan on the delivery of the case of rifles as he had agreed before. But as he spoke, his mind was also working on another plan, one that made him grin at the thought. It was a plan, that if done right, would result in more money in his pocket, a fine time with a couple of women, and no sharing with the others. He chuckled to himself as he thought about what he hoped would happen.

B ull was angry; angry with Big Spotted Horse, angry
with the captain and the others, and angry with
himself. Never one to willingly take orders from anyone,
the big man had bullied his way through life and so far,
that had served him well. He had usually managed to
come out on top of any dealings with others, whether by
brain or brawn, usually the latter. But when he was up
against an entire war party of Pawnee, who were determined to get their way in the trade, he had to step back
and consider his options, and they were few. He was
mulling things over as he rode back toward the wagons,
knowing he would have to confront the captain to get
the rifles for the Pawnee. When the first wagon came in
sight, Bull spotted the captain and another rider out
front, talking as they rode and as they neared, Bull
recognized the major, the man that had put this expedition together. What he did not know was if the major
knew anything about the rifles for the Sioux.

Bull reined up to wait for them, moving off the trail
and leaning forward to rest on the pommel of his saddle
as he waited. When they neared, he said, "Got a good site

all picked out for ya', Cap'n. Just a little ways further, near the trees and close to water."

"Good, good. Any problems?" asked the captain, glancing from Bull to the major.

"Nuthin' we can't take care of, Cap'n," responded Bull, nodding with his head that he wasn't anxious to speak in front of the major.

"That's alright, Bull, the major knows everything. Fact is, he planned most of it."

Bull slowly lifted his head, sat up straight in his saddle. "No problems, less'n you count about twenty Pawnee warriors, painted for war, a problem."

"What?! Where?!" he asked, standing in his stirrups to look past the big man.

"They're in the trees yonder, waitin' for a case of rifles an' some ammunition."

"The same ones you dealt with before?" asked the captain, his anger showing red about his neck and rising to his face.

"Ummhmm, Big Spotted Horse and his boys," casually replied Bull, leaning forward on his pommel again.

"I suppose you made some arrangements with him?"

"That's right. After we camp, he an' his boys'll come in the trees, we give 'em the rifles, everything easy as you please."

"One case?"

"That's right. One case, an' some ammunition."

The captain looked at the major who had sat quiet through the exchange, but the glare on his face said more than his words. "You take care of this, Captain, or I will!" growled the major, reining his horse around to return to the wagons.

The captain scowled at Bull. "This will come out of your share!"

73

"Ummhmm, thot you'd say that. We'll see," answered Bull, looking back up the trail and to the trees where he expected to find the Pawnee.

REUBEN SAT CROSS-LEGGED BESIDE THE GNARLY CEDAR, binoculars lifted as he watched the three men on the trail, and even at this distance, he could tell it was not a friendly interchange. When the man he recognized as the major turned away and started back to the wagons, he saw the threatening gestures made by the captain and knew there was more than a little trouble brewing. He had already guessed the motives of Big Spotted Horse and knew he and his warriors would not leave without the rifles, but Reuben wondered if the trade would take place peacefully or if the bunch at the wagons would do something to rile the chief. As he watched the men turn back to the wagons, he thought, *Reckon I'll have to get close to the wagons again, watch what happens. Maybe I can keep Spotted Horse from wiping out the train.*

He had mounted the scope on his Sharps, thinking he would need it for long range shooting if the Pawnee attacked the train, but knowing he would be close, he started removing the scope and planned on keeping the Henry close at hand. A glance to the sky told him the wagons would be nearing and whatever the Pawnee and the big man from the wagons had planned would soon be taking place. He knew he would need to be closer to the wagons, especially after nightfall, to be able to intervene or help, if necessary, but he still did not want to reveal himself to the others, for some reason he believed there was still more planned with the cases of rifles. He had hoped that Bridger would return, but with no sign of the mountain man, he had to make his own plans.

The binoculars brought him close enough to watch the activities of the families and the wagons. The big Conestoga took a similar place near the trees, with the tail gate end within a few paces of the trees. Most wagon masters would tell his people to stay further away, eliminating the opportunity of any attackers sneaking close, but the position of the wagon told Reuben what was planned with the Pawnee. He searched the area, the rolling flats of the plains, the tree line, every possible approach he would have once the curtain of darkness lay upon the flats.

The wagons were circled, the animals kept within the circle, and several families were lighting their cookfires when Reuben left his promontory and returned to his horse and mule. He fashioned a leather thong sling for the Henry, checked the loads of both the rifle and his pistol, as well as the spare cylinder of the Remington. He donned his uniform dark green wool frock coat, put a handful of cartridges for the Henry in his pocket, and started from his camp on foot, choosing to be as stealthy and as invisible as possible. Whenever the dip of the land offered cover, he moved in a crouch, but much of the way, he was on hands and knees, keeping below the height of spring growth grasses.

Most of an hour passed as he worked his way toward the riverside trees, just over a mile across the grassy plains, and as he entered the trees, he smelled horses. The sweat and droppings were distinctive, and too close to be the animals of the wagons. Reuben slowly rose to his feet amidst a cluster of cottonwoods and dogwood. The sounds of the horses were nearer the water, their snorting and nickering masked by the sounds of the river, but Reuben waited for other movement, knowing the Pawnee would not be far from their horses. Movement caught his attention, or rather the deep shadow of movement. The moon was waning from full and was less than three quarters, but the moonlight pierced the canopy of trees, showing dim lances of light and stretching the shadows of any moving creature. As he watched, three figures were slowly moving closer to the wagons, and he guessed the bigger man in the lead was Big Spotted Horse. But Reuben moved nothing but his eyes, slowing his shallow breathing as he watched.

The sycamore trees near the edge of the tree line behind the big Conestoga, kept the wagon in darkness, with the cookfires of the wagons seeming to magnify the darkness, casting shadows into the trees. But the grunting and huffing of men, the sliding of something heavy across the lowered tailgate, told Reuben of the actions of the men of the wagon. They were unloading at least one case of rifles, perhaps more.

The whispered greeting from one of the traders, probably the big man, Bull, brought Big Spotted Horse closer. Bull was easily distinguished with his girth and thick beard, highlighted by thin shafts of moonlight, as he spoke softly to Spotted Horse. "Ya got the money?"

Reuben watched as the chief handed a heavy pouch to Bull, who hefted the leather bag, and showed his savvy by accepting the chief's offering. "I got one case of rifles and two boxes of ammo, as you asked. Now this finishes our deal an' you an' yore men are hightailin' it outta here, right?" he growled.

Spotted Horse motioned to the men with him, and they stacked the smaller boxes of ammo on top the larger case of rifles, bent to grab the rope handles at the end of the crate and grunting as they lifted, started into the deeper trees. Reuben heard Spotted Horse, "We are done! If those are not what you said, we will come and take every rifle from those with you in the wagons!"

"Don't go threatenin' me!" growled Bull, stepping toward the chief.

But Spotted Horse did not flinch or back away, only answered, "I do not threaten!" The chief turned away, showing his back to the white men, and stalked after his men.

Bull growled at the others, "The cap'n said he wants this," slapping the pouch of coins that hung at his belt and started past the men as they lifted the tailgate of the wagon to seal off the cargo.

Bugs nodded his white mane to Bull but turned to Zeke as the big man stomped off, "We better follow him. I wouldn't trust him with a nickel, much less six hunert dollars!"

"Si, si. Me neither," answered the wiry haired Mexican.

B ull stomped past the Conestoga, stepped over the downed tongue and into the light of the circle of wagons. With his thumbs in his belt, he hoisted his britches as he looked around the circle, spotted what he searched for and turned back to move past the Conestoga to the wagons behind. With the rotating of wagons on their position among the train, he was looking for what had been the lead wagon of the day. It was the woman at the cookfire, her blonde hair showing in the firelight, that caught his attention and prompted his move in that direction. As he passed the fire beside the Conestoga, he saw only the couple that handled the wagon at the cookfire. Oscar, 'Butch' Newberry, and the woman that acted as his wife, Cora, the redheaded tavern woman recruited by the captain. He chuckled to himself, thinking his plan was going just as he wanted. With the captain and major away from the wagon, there would be no one to interfere. He had already taken his horse and another to just inside the tree line, saddled and ready.

The *thunk* of metal hitting wood was a common

sound when people were cutting wood for their fires, but this was a little different. George Betts had been a butcher, with his own small but successful shop in southern Michigan, when he and his family decided to get away from the war and move to the west. Now he was butchering a couple deer taken by one of the scouts to be shared among the families on the train. Major Pendergrast had asked him to do the butchering, making bundles that could be distributed to the families and he had just finished one deer, sunk the blade of his cleaver in the wood plank and bent to fetch the second carcass, when a growl from near the fire caught his attention.

George Betts turned to see the big back of Bull, the lead scout for the wagons, standing between him and his wife who was busy at the cookfire. "Here, here! What do you want? Is it the meat, I'm done with one," he turned slightly to motion to the meat bundles wrapped in pieces of hide that lay beside his plank bench.

Bull turned to snarl at the man, "Stay outta this, it don't concern you!" and turned back to the blonde wife of the man. He cackled as he sneered at her, the corner of his lip lifting, "You 'n me are gonna have us a good time. I got'chu a horse over yonder, an' you're comin' with me!"

"I am not! Get away from me, you filthy brute!" retorted the woman, trying to look past the big man to her husband. "George!"

Bull grabbed at Mabel as she tried to run past him, catching her around the waist and jerking her off her feet, holding her like a sack under his arm. The movement turned him toward George who stood frozen, eyes wide, as he started to reach for his wife. Bull cackled and stepped close to the man, pulling the woman closer as she tried to hit and kick him. He smashed his flat palm against the face of George, turned slightly as if leaving and swung his meaty forearm in a back hand and knocked the much smaller George, back against the plank bench, knocking him, the bench, the meat, and tools into a pile. Bull leaned over, snarled at George who was struggling out from under the deer carcass and more, "If you know what's good fer ya, you'll stay right there till we're gone!"

As Bull started away from the cookfire, the teen daughter, Madeline came from around the wagon, stopped with wide eyes and put her hand to her mouth when she saw her mother struggling under the big man's arm. Bull reached out for the girl, as she ducked away from his reach. But Bull was determined and grabbed a handful of the girl's hair, jerked her back off her feet. "You're comin' with us, little missy!" as the girl started screaming at the beast that grabbed her. Bull jerked at her hair. "Hush up!" he growled, and tried to get a better grip on the girl.

Reuben had heard the ruckus and was quietly making his way closer. He stopped at the corner of the Betts wagon and saw the back of Bull and the women struggling to free themselves. He lifted his rifle, leaning against the wagon, looking for a clear shot, but the women were kicking, clawing, screaming and from Reuben's angle, he dared not shoot at the three that were tangled together.

The flash of light, the *thrum, thrum,* of sound gave Reuben an instant of thought that a bird of prey was swooping down, but the next sound was the same as a bursting watermelon, or that of an axe buried in a stump. Bull crumpled to his knees, losing his grip on the women, and the flash of light reflected off the blade of the thrown cleaver showed the blade was buried deep in the back of Bull's head as the big man fell onto his face, never to move again.

The women scrambled to their feet, both glancing down at the man, fear showing in their eyes under wrinkled brows. Both turned back to see their husband and father, standing spread legged, arms hanging at his side as his chin dropped to his heaving chest. They turned back to look again at the buried meat cleaver, looked back at George Betts, the peace-loving man that hated violence so much he uprooted his family to flee the war, and ran to his arms, overflowing with gratitude and pride in the quiet man.

The ruckus had attracted several others and they came near to see what had happened, looking from the gruesome sight of the bloodied head and neck of the dead Bull, and back at the family still embracing one another. The major and captain came from further up the line and stepped into the firelight. The captain went close to the dead Bull, dropped to one knee beside him, hid his actions by his body and removed the satchel of coins. He stood and looked back at George Betts. "You're gonna pay for this. Out here the only law is the law of the wagons, and nobody can murder another without paying the price!" He stood to his feet, shaking his head. "I don't care who you are, nobody kills one of my men!"

"But, but," started Mabel, looking from her husband to the major and the captain.

"No buts about it! There's no denying that's the butcher's cleaver in that man's head, and it's also clear he struck him from the back. That's the same as shooting a man in the back and that deserves hanging!" his voice raised as he spoke and gestured threateningly, moving closer to the three that hugged one another protectively.

The captain looked at the gathering crowd, "Anybody

here see what happened?" He looked from one to another, waiting for someone to speak up. "Just like I thought!" He looked at Bugs and Zeke, who had followed, saw some of what happened and also saw the captain take the coin pouch. "You two, get that man ready for hanging!"

"Now hold on!" interjected the major. "There should be a trial, at least," he protested.

"We just had our trial! You saw it, ain't nobody seen it and we can't take the word of his wife and kid, they'd say anything to save his neck!"

The major stepped back, lowered his eyes to the ground, unwilling to look at the others, and by his acquiescence, gave permission to the others to take the man.

"I saw it!" came a voice from the darkness between the wagons. Everyone froze, looking to see who was talking, as Reuben stepped from behind the wagon of the Betts family. Holding his cocked rifle in the crook of his arm, his hand on the stock and finger on the trigger, he stepped into the firelight, standing at a slight angle, the muzzle of his rifle pointed at the three men. "I can tell you exactly what happened, Major, if you want the truth!"

The major seemed to perk up and lifted his head. "Of course, of course. We want the truth."

"The truth is, if this man," nodding to George Betts, "had not thrown his cleaver when he did, I would have shot that man down before he got any further. You see, he had grabbed this man's wife, knocked him back against his table and knockin' everything to the ground. Told him he was takin' his wife and would kill him if he followed. And when the girl there," nodding to the daughter, "came around the wagon, he grabbed her and was goin' to take her too. What this man did was the same as what any man here would do; he protected his family, and whether here or in the city, there is no law against that!"

"Who're you, and why should we take your word for what happened? I don't believe you!" growled the captain and motioned to his men to get the stranger.

Reuben saw the white-haired man look his way and lift his rifle toward him, but Reuben swung his rifle at his hip and the Henry blasted. The man's face splattered as the bullet smashed his nose, driving through his head and taking a fist sized chunk of meat and bone out the back of his neck, driving him to his back where he flopped spread-eagled and lay completely still.

The shot had startled everyone present, freezing them in place with the sudden violence, but the visitor jacked another cartridge into the chamber as he swung his rifle toward the Mexican. "Don't do it," warned Reuben. The wiry man grinned, nodding, holding his hands wide as if surrendering. Reuben glanced away to see what the captain was doing, but his peripheral vision caught Zeke's sudden movement as he reached behind his neck to grab his knife, and Reuben's rifle spoke its message of death again.

Within moments, three of the five gun traders were dead. The people mumbled to one another, each one afraid to move. But Reuben spoke again, "As I was sayin', the reason you can believe what I say, is because I also saw these men sell a case of illegal Springfield rifles and two boxes of ammunition to the Pawnee war party that waited in the woods behind us. It just so happens that I know the chief of the Pawnee, Big Spotted Horse, and I knew that man," nodding to the body of Bull, "and his friends had tried to cheat the chief out of their fair trade and put this entire wagon train in danger of an attack. If any of you know anythin' about trackin', you're free to go back there in the woods, examine the sign, and you'll see I'm right. But you are not in danger now, the Pawnee left after they got their rifles. Now it remains for you to decide what you as a group, want to do about that man," pointing with his rifle to driver of the Conestoga, "and the captain there about what they plan to do with the rest of the rifles in that wagon."

"Now hold on! I don't know nothin' 'bout no rifles! I ain't got nuthin' to do with all that!" pleaded the captain, looking from Reuben to the crowd that was now showing their anger with the traitorous bunch.

The major stepped forward; he was fuming at the way things had turned against them, but he was a man used to controlling any situation he was presented. With added resolve, he breathed deep and with hands uplifted. "Now, folks, settle down, settle down. We don't know this man, but if what he says is true, the greatest threat is dead!" he pointed to the three bodies that lay nearby. "If there is anything else we need to be concerned about, we'll take care of it in due time. Now, I suggest you all go back to your wagons, and we'll deal with this in the daylight."

The people looked from one to the other, talking among themselves, and as is so often true with people, it is easier to put unpleasant things out of mind when they can be dealt with at another time. After all, most think that no decision is better than a wrong decision. As the crowd turned away, someone called out, "Where'd he go?" pointing to the wagon where their visitor had stood and was now nowhere to be seen.

R euben forked his roan, grabbed up the lead of the mule and started into the clear night. It was cool enough for Reuben to keep his wool frock coat about him and settle deep into his saddle, one hand on the reins the other clasping the collar of the coat closed. He pulled the floppy brim of his hat down over his forehead, hunkered into his coat, peering out at the waving grasses bouncing the moonlight off their silvery shafts. He glanced at the stars, calculated the time by the big dipper and knew it was a little past midnight, allowing him several hours on the trail before the wagons took to the ruts.

He thought about the confrontation with the major and his captain, knowing they were just as involved in the selling of the rifles to the Indians as were the three dead men, and wondered what story they would present to the people to keep them moving west. But people that are full of hopes and dreams and have burned the bridges behind them are not easily dissuaded from their purpose and Reuben was certain the entire train would be on the trail at first light. He often found it amazing and even amusing how easily people can be convinced to do whatever suits their purpose, right or wrong, and the wrong easily justified. He knew many lived by the adage that the end justifies the means, but he also knew grave-yards were full of those 'justifications'.

The Oregon trail and the Overland trail established by the Pony Express and the Overland Stage, followed the same trail from Fort Kearny to the forks of the North and South Platte Rivers. They had passed several of the stage stations that had taken over for the Pony Express, and some that had been abandoned. Just yesterday, a stage had passed the wagon train, making its way to the west and ultimately California, but Reuben did not expect to see any other stagecoaches, at least for a day or two, yet he might stop at one of the stations for an update on any Indian uprisings.

The light in the window was just snuffed out as the dim light of early morning struggled to chase the dark-ness from the land. Reuben rode up to the squared log building that was sided by a small barn and corrals that held several mules, probably teams for the stages, and a couple horses. He hailed the station, "Helloo the house!" and saw the front door open a crack and a rifle barrel protrude.

"Come on, if'n yore friendly!" came an answer.

Reuben grinned, nudged the roan close and asked, "Alright if I get down?"

"Shore, only keep yore hands clear o' any weepons!"

Reuben chuckled, stepped down and slapped the rein of the roan over the hitch rail, followed by the lead of the mule, loosened their girths and turned to the man at the door. "Bridger said this is a good place to resupply, that right?"

"It be. Bridger, you say? Where'd you see him?"

"A few days back on the trail goin' to Fort Kearny."

"Come on in then, coffee pot's on."

As Reuben stepped through the door, he was surprised to see the large room filled with barrels, boxes, bags, and bins of goods. Shelves lined the back wall behind the plank counter that was no more than two planks atop two barrels, three tables with chairs and stools filled the room.

"Take a seat, I'll bring the coffee, we'll sit a spell."

When the man returned, he held the coffee pot in one hand, two tin cups in the other. He sat the cups down, poured them full of fresh steaming java and sat the pot down, extending his hand.

"I'm Sam Machette, this here's muh place. Been here a while 'fore the pony boys came thru, now we're holdin' stock fer the stages, feed the passengers when they got some, trade with folks on the wagons and such when they stop."

"Sounds like you're stayin' busy," replied Reuben, accepting the offered hand, "I'm Reuben Grundy, headin' west."

Machette sat down, pulled his cup close, looked over the rim at Reuben, "I recognize your duds as some kinda uniform. Been in the war, have ya?"

"Yup. Served with Berdan's Sharpshooters, took some lead, got out and now I'm gettin' as far from it as I can," explained Reuben.

"Cain't say's I blame ya. Young feller like yourself oughta be gettin' you a woman, settlin' down, raisin' a bunch o' young'uns."

Reuben chuckled. "I'm too young to get hitched. Got too much country to see first."

"Got the wanderlust has ya?" replied Machette. "I had

it, that's why I come out'chere amongst the Injuns, thot I'd found Nirvana. Got muh wife, she's in the back, purty young thing, and got a Irish cook. She ain't so purty, but she shore can cook, and them folks on the stage shore like stoppin' here. I think them drivers kinda time their stoppin' so they can get her vittles." He laughed at the thought, thinking of the many stages and passengers that had been through.

Reuben sipped the coffee, looked up at Machette. "Any problem with Indians?"

"Me? Nah. Ain't had much trouble, they like comin' in an' tradin' fer stuff. But I been hearin' things from some o' the Cheyenne, talkin' 'bout the Sioux."

"What do you hear?"

"Seems there's a handful o' young bucks that're itchin' for a fight. One o' the leaders is a son of the Lakota chief Black Fox; his name is Kickin' Bear. Him an' his brothers, Flyin' Hawk and young Black Fox, have been stirrin' up the young warriors. They got other family, cousins or sumpin', Eagle Thunder and Walkin' Eagle, that have been followin' 'em and make up a pretty tough bunch all by themselves."

"Do they trade with you?"

"Most o' the Sioux, Cheyenne, 'rapaho, some Pawnee, all come in here, time to time. I keep a good stock o' things they want, you know, beads, sugar, pots, knives and such."

"You trade rifles with 'em?"

Machette leaned back, looking at Reuben skeptically. "You think I'm crazy or sumpin'? Even it were legal, ain't no way I'd put a rifle in their hands. Why, I'd as soon pour coal oil all over muh cabin and muh own self and strike a spark! That wouldn't kill me any faster'n givin' them rifles. The onliest thing keepin' 'em from killin' ever white man around is that the sojer boys and them folks on the wagons have all got rifles an' such, but even then they hit some o' them wagons just to get their hands on a white man's weapons!" He paused, shaking his head at the thought. "No sir, that'd be plumb crazy!"

"That's what Bridger said, and that's what I was thinkin', and yet there's those that are more interested in makin' money than the lives of families and more that travel through the Indians' territory," added Reuben, finishing his coffee just as a young woman came from the back.

"Well, lookee here. C'mon oer' here sweet thing," said Machette, waving at the young woman. As she came near, he slipped his arm around her waist and drew her close, smiling at her and looking at Reuben, "Sweetie, this here's Reuben. Reuben, this here's muh wife, Susan."

Reuben stood, doffed his hat, and nodded. "Pleased to meet'chu, ma'am."

She smiled. "Pleased to meet you, Reuben." She looked down at her husband. "You hungry?"

He chuckled.

"Have you ever known me not to be hungry?"

"Lucy has some hot biscuits, duck eggs, bacon, and fried potatoes."

"Bring us both a big plate, if you please," answered Machette, nodding to Reuben.

AS THE MEN FINISHED THEIR FOOD, SUSAN BROUGHT MORE coffee and the men sat back to enjoy the black brew. Machette looked at Reuben. "When you asked about tradin' rifles, I reckoned you was askin' fer a partik'lar reason. What's on your mind, youngster?"

"Youngster?" asked Reuben, chuckling. "It's been a

long time since anybody called me youngster. Actually, it was just 'fore I left home to join up, and that's what my Pa called me." He shook his head, his eyes glazing with the thought of his father, then looked up at Machette. "But to answer your question, yes, there's a particular reason. There's a wagon train about a day behind me, not a big one, just fifteen wagons. But there's a big Conestoga packin' several cases of 'Bibles' and 'Farm tools', at least that's what the letterin' on the boxes says. But I had a chance to crack 'em open and found they are Springfield rifles and several boxes of ammunition."

"You don't say," grumbled the trader, frowning and showing anger flaring in his eyes as he gritted his teeth, flexing his jaw muscles. "If the women folks weren't close, I'd be cussin' an' turnin' the air blue!" he growled. He looked up at Reuben. "I take it you got some kind o' plan to put a stop to that?"

"No plan, but I'm gonna do whatever I can to stop it. They traded one case to a Pawnee chief, Big Spotted Horse, back down the trail, but that was legal accordin' to the colonel. Seems they've recruited several Pawnee as scouts and the Pawnee been friendly with most folks. But near as I can tell, this bunch wants to trade with some of these Indians further from the fort, and I'm thinkin' they've made a deal with this fella you mentioned, Kickin' Bear."

"You can't let 'em give them rifles to that man! He'll turn 'em against every wagon train that comes through here and he'll prob'ly go against Fort Laramie and all the stage stations, including this'n."

"Well, I'm not sure what to do yet, but...say, you have any Sharps cartridges? Or some for the Remington .44?"

"I do, and you can have all you need, if you'll use 'em to stop them gunrunners!" He quickly stood, turned to the shelves, and started gathering the boxes of paper cartridges, turned to look at Reuben. "You need anythin' else?"

"Cartridges for a Henry .44?"

"Got 'em!"

"The next station is Cottonwood Springs, 'bout fifteen miles, near the confluence of the north and south branches o' the Platte. You might get'chu some more information 'bout the Sioux from them; they done more tradin' with 'em than me. Now, if'n you keep to the north branch, that's whar the wagon trail goes, ain't no more stage stations till ya' get to the mountains. But if'n I was lookin' to find the Sioux, their territory is north o' the river, and 'bout a good day's ride from the confluence, the Birdwood crick comes from the north, splits them dryland hills, and right 'bout there I reckon you'll find some Sioux, back up that crick a spell."

Samuel Machette stood leaning against the hitchrail, watching Reuben stash his new supply of cartridges in the panier aboard the mule. Legs crossed at the ankles, arms folded over his chest, he spat a wad of tobacco, wiped his face with his sleeve, and added, "I met Kickin' Bear last year, him an' his friends brought in some buffler hides to trade and he tried to get a rifle then, but I keep the few I got outta sight and tol' him I didn't have none. He weren't too happy 'bout that an' after huffin' 'n' puffin' a mite, they left with a couple new knives, a hatchet, an' some gewgaws fer their womenfolk. But he ain't no one I'd wanna tangle with, that's fer shore."

Reuben tightened the girths on the horse and mule, stepped aboard and started to rein away when Machette asked, "Ya want me to be sayin' anythin' to them folks in the wagons?"

"No, if they think the Sioux are comin' down on 'em, no tellin' what they'd do, and far as I know, the Indians have no such intent. I reckon they're just after the rifles and such."

"Don't go taken them Oglala Sioux fer granted, if'n them young bucks are thinkin' war, they won't hesitate a wit to take a scalp or two. Wouldn't s'prise me none to see 'em take them rifles and scalp the one whut brought 'em." He shifted his weight, stood tall and watched as Reuben reined away, he hollered after him, "Keep yore hair on!"

"You, too!" answered Reuben, chuckling as he started to the trail. The sun was at his back and his shadow stretched long before him. Although they had traveled most of the night, the animals had a short rest and were eager for the trail and the roan stretched out, his head bobbing slightly with his gait and the mule stayed close, not to be outdone by his short-eared friend. The saddle was a good place for thinking and Reuben set his mind to the problem of the gun runners. He was determined to keep the rifles from the Indians, especially since they were apparently bound for the restive Sioux and a bunch of young bucks that were anxious for honors and scalps. Reuben lifted one eyebrow, as he slowly looked around, searching for any sign of trouble. He thought he could not really fault the young bucks, after all, he felt much the same when he left home for the war; intent on getting into the fight and maybe get a medal or two, maybe a promotion, make his family proud. He never really thought that to earn those honors, others would have to die at his hand, and when it came to killing, he had proven himself very capable and that began to bother him. He was almost relieved when he fell under the fire of the grey coats, taking two bullets and putting him out of the fight. But the killing had not stopped, but he had no choice in each of the fights he was forced into, and now it appeared he would once again have to put men in his sights to save the lives of others. Would it never end?

He thought on the words of his father, not unlike the words of the pastor in their little church in White Pigeon, *As long as there is evil in the world, good men will be forced to take a stand against it, and that means being willing to do the worst to save the best.* And his father had made it clear, to do the worst did not mean stooping to the level of evil, but to do whatever is necessary to stand for the right, even if it meant killing in that defense.

Reuben breathed deep, focusing on the terrain before and around him, always watchful for danger, but also for game. And movement in the low swale caught his eye as he reined up for a better look. A big bull buffalo was walking from the low end, slowly making his way toward the river, his ponderous head swinging side to side, his beard dragging in the grass. He was a majestic sight, surprising Reuben as the bull paid him no mind, focused on the trees and the river beyond. He had thought of taking some meat for the people of the wagons, but the bull was more than he wanted, thinking a deer would better suffice. He knew the work required to skin and butcher a big bull and it would take two to three hours, maybe more, and the sun would be high on his back and the meat could start to spoil before the wagons came near. He grinned, sat still as the monarch of the plains ambled across the flats and disappeared into the trees.

It was a little past midday when the station came in sight, and it was a structure that contrasted with the terrain thereabouts. Rising two stories high, the cedar log building had a peaked roof, covered with shake shingles, a novelty for the wilderness such as this, but impressive to the many travelers on the stagecoaches. Originally a stop for the pony express, the McDonald ranch now served as a stagecoach stop, trading post for travelers and Indians alike, and a way station for wagon trains. It stood regally overlooking the narrow Cottonwood creek, and from the upper stories, one could easily see both forks of the Platte. Both the creek and the river were thick with cottonwoods, willows, and sycamore, with ample underbrush of serviceberry and choke cherry. The tall trees near the building offered shade, depending on the time of day, and from one big branch of an oak, hung a board-bottomed swing, but no children were seen about.

The corrals behind the store building were thick logs, making for a fortress for the animals, or men as the necessity required. The fences extended to the arroyo that abutted the canyon with the creek, and at the end of the corral, another log structure served as barn and blacksmith shop. Reuben rode up to the corrals, stepped down and let his animals take water at the trough that extended from the corral. He rested one arm on the pole fence as he looked around and was hailed by a man coming from the barn, "Afternoon! Passin' through, are ye?"

"Ummhmm. Thought I'd see 'bout gettin' sumpin' to eat, chew the fat a little."

"Come on in, coffee's always on and I'll see if I can get the missus to put somethin' in the pot. I'm McDonald," offered the man, nodding to Reuben who responded with, "I'm Reuben Grundy."

"Well, come on in, Reuben, and welcome."

He stepped through the door, stood to the side for a moment for his eyes to become accustomed to the dim light, a practice he learned since he left the army, and looked around at the well-stocked interior. It was similar to the one operated by Machette, but larger and better stocked. There were four tables with chairs, the counter was well built, and the shelves covered two walls with barrels, crates and more stacked elsewhere. McDonald motioned him to come to the table that stood alone in the sunlight, the shafts of light showing the dust in the air and the fly specks on the window. Reuben took the offered chair, saw the steaming cup of coffee, and lifted it to his lips and took a long draught. "Umm, that's good coffee!" he declared, appreciatively.

"That's my wife's doin', she's good at everythin' in the kitchen. She'll bring us a plate soon." McDonald paused, looking at Reuben's clothing, recognizing it as uniform style, and asked, "Ain't never seen a green uniform; was that from the war?"

"Ummhmmm, Union, Berdan's Sharpshooters. They thought we needed a bit better camouflage since we spent most of the time sneakin' through the woods."

The silver-haired McDonald frowned, sipping his coffee, and looking at Reuben over his cup. "You don't hardly look old enough to have been in the war and out here on your own."

"I'm not, but here I am," replied Reuben, chuckling and grinning, lifting his cup again.

McDonald laughed. "I reckon war is a young man's game, such as it is."

"When a man gets weighted down with lead, it kinda ages him."

"Reckon it does," mulled the older man.

"I understand you been runnin' this station and tradin' house for some time, that right?" asked Reuben, looking around the premises at the goods.

"Ummhmm, been about four, five years now. Started it as a tradin' post, then the pony express came through, now the stage line. All the while the Indians been comin' in, time to time."

"Bridger says he thinks the Sioux might be talkin' war. What do you think?"

"When were you talkin' to Bridger?"

"Couple days back, we passed on the trail. He was bound for the fort."

The older man breathed deep, swirled the last of his coffee in his cup and looked up at Reuben. "It sure looks like it. There's some young ones that are stirrin' things up."

"Kickin' Bear?"

The storekeeper frowned. "You know about Kickin' Bear?"

"From Bridger," nodded Reuben. "Have you seen the Sioux lately?"

"Not for a while. Haven't heard much, either. Usually the stages bring news with 'em, but none of 'em said much, lately." He shook his head as he frowned, sitting his cup down and looking toward the kitchen, expecting his wife with the food.

He looked at Reuben, spoke softly, "Don't let my woman hear you talkin' 'bout the Sioux. I think she knows there's trouble brewin', but I don't want her gettin' all bothered 'bout somethin' we have no control over."

"I understand. But I need your help," started Reuben, and continued to tell the trader about the wagon of rifles and what he thought they intended. When he asked about a likely spot a trade like that would happen, he answered, "Birdwood creek. That's the way they come down from the north where most of their people are durin' the summer months. The headwater of that creek is where the buffalo grounds start." He looked at Reuben. "But how you gonna stop it?"

"Don't rightly know yet, but I'm open to suggestions." Before McDonald could respond both men saw the woman coming from the kitchen, her arms loaded with dishes and a broad smile on her face.

The men smiled, stood as she came to the table and as she sat the plates and platters down, McDonald said, "Reuben, this is the little lady, Margarite. Margarite, this is Reuben Grundy, just passing through."

The woman showed slightly greying hair, sun tanned skin, laugh wrinkles at the corner of her eyes and mouth, and still showed a firm figure. She smiled, wiped her hands on her apron, and extended her wrinkled hand. "Pleased to meet you, Reuben Grundy, just passing through."

"Pleased, ma'am. And thank you for this fine feast!" declared Reuben, waving his hand over the bounty. She turned away, leaving the men to their food, and glanced over her shoulder as she entered the kitchen. Reuben looked at McDonald. "You're a lucky man, and she's a fine lady."

"She is that, and I am indeed a lucky man. That's what

concerns me. We've been friends with the Oglala, the Cheyenne, Arapaho and the Pawnee, but when them young bucks start talkin' war, ain't nobody gonna be safe." Reuben only nodded, more intent on the platters of food before him.

A s they were finishing their meal, another man stepped through the door, looked at McDonald, "Another train rollin' in, but they be acrost the river. An' I spotted a stage, couple miles out, comin' from the east."

McDonald nodded, glanced at Reuben, "That's the blacksmith, Roscoe Hindman. Been here couple years now, they keep him busy."

Reuben looked at the man who had already turned away and stepped outside. The door stood ajar, and he could be seen standing, shading his eyes and looking toward the river. He looked back to the men at the table, "Looks to be 'bout twenty or so wagons. They're on the Mormon trail, but that don't mean nuthin'."

McDonald raised his voice, "We'll just hafta wait'n see. Might not even stop, less'n they circle up for the night."

Only a grunt came from the smithy who dropped his hand and turned back to his work at the barn. Reuben looked to McDonald and asked, "Is there room in the barn for me to stretch out my blankets for the night?"

"Certainly, certainly. But you don't hafta rush off right yet," replied the storekeeper.

"Well, figger I'll get settled 'fore the stage comes in, maybe talk to the driver 'bout seein' any Indians."

"Good idea. I'll quiz 'em a little also."

THE STAGE MADE THEIR STOP FOR THE NIGHT, THREE passengers, a man and a middle-aged couple, would bunk down in the main building, while the driver and shotgun guard would take to the barn. When the stage group had finished their meal, a hail from outside brought McDonald to the door to see five riders followed by a single wagon. The leader spoke up, "I'm Lorenzo Stenhouse, captain of the train across the way," nodding toward the far side of the river. "You've still got a blacksmith here, do ya?"

"That's right, his shop is back in the barn," motioned McDonald from the front stoop of the store.

"We also have a list of supplies we need," stated Stenhouse, digging in his pocket for a prepared list for the wagons. "It'll probably take the smithy half-day or so to fix the wheels and gear we brought over, then we'll load the supplies on the wagon, so there's no hurry," he leaned forward to hand the list to McDonald.

The storekeeper took the list, looked it over, glanced up at Stenhouse, "Shouldn't be any problem puttin' this together." He looked at the other riders, "You fellas hungry? We've always got extra!"

The men looked at one another, nodding and grinning as they nudged their horses to the hitchrail while the captain motioned the wagon to go to the smithy's. Margarite had come from the store with her husband, and with a glance to him, she turned back inside to ready the meal for the newcomers. The men from the train took their seats at two tables, the five riders and the two on the wagon, but their leader set the example as they doffed their hats and bowed together for prayer.

When they finished, they were cheerful and talkative as McDonald took a chair, turned it around and straddled the seat, resting his arms of the tall back. He spoke to the leader, "You folks Mormon?" It was a simple question, and he showed friendliness as he asked.

Stenhouse glanced at McDonald, slowly smiled. "We are with the LDS church, yes."

"We had others that have passed through, some comin', some goin'. I understand that your leaders have sent wagons back from the west to help folks make the journey, that right?"

"Yes. We came out last fall, helped several of the faithful to dispose of the remaining properties and prepare for the journey. We are now on our way to join the others."

McDonald smiled, nodding his understanding. "Your people come from far?"

"Some have come from as far away as Europe, but those on this train were living in Iowa. We have folks from Plum Hollow, Pleasant Grove, Mt. Pisgah, Macedonia, Kanesville and others. This will probably be the last train of our faithful."

"Well, you folks might want to be extra careful, seems the Oglala Sioux are a bit restive. Seems some of their young warriors are stirrin' up some trouble with so many folks passing through their lands. Our stages keep us up on what's been happenin' back along the trail," explained McDonald.

Stenhouse looked from the storekeeper to the other men and back. "We had a little run-in with some Pawnee back along the trail a couple days ago, but it was just a few trying to steal some horses. Our men were vigilant and ran them off without our losing any stock."

"That's good, but the Sioux are a little more war-savvy than the Pawnee. Many of the Pawnee have been peaceful with the settlers and soldiers, some have even become scouts for the soldiers, but the Sioux, well, they're not as friendly."

"Thank you for the warning, Mr. McDonald. We will make it a point to be extra vigilant, but I believe we have sufficient arms to properly defend ourselves."

"Been in an Injun fight have ya?" asked the storekeeper.

"Just the little fracas with the Pawnee horse thieves. But I'm sure it will be no different with any other Native people, when they see our resolve and our weapons, they will probably flee like the others."

McDonald just looked at the man, sighed heavily and shrugged as he stood. There was much he wanted to say, but he had met people like this man before and talking to them was like beating your head against an empty barrel, might make noise but accomplish nothing. He walked back to the kitchen area where his wife was finishing the last of the dishes for the men's meal. He glanced at her, she recognized the expression and shook her head, knowing the frustration her husband felt when people were so intentionally ignorant and arrogant even to the endangering of the lives of others. "I'm goin' to the barn to talk to Reuben," he declared, leaving her and her helper to the task of serving the meal.

Reuben had been talking with the driver and shotgun messenger that came in on the stagecoach, but quickly learned with their route following the South Platte, their contact with the Sioux had been very limited, but the

Arapaho were prevalent along most of their route. He was getting ready to stretch out his blankets when McDonald came from the house and motioned him to the big front door of the barn. As Reuben came close, McDonald turned and pointed to the root cellar behind the house. "In the root cellar yonder, I keep the kegs and barrels of black powder. When we were talkin' 'bout that Conestoga with the rifles, it got me to thinkin'. Most wagons have a hammock of sorts that hang under the wagons for when they gotta gather buff'lo chips for fire. Folks walk alongside, pick up the chips and toss 'em into the hammock under the wagon an' when they stop, they have their supply all set." He looked at Reuben to see if he was understanding, and as Reuben slowly nodded, he continued. "If'n you were to sneak in after dark and put one o' them kegs of powder in that hammock, then later..."

Reuben chuckled, almost laughing as he shook his head, "Then later, BOOM!" he declared. He took a deep breath, "But I thought black powder had to have a spark, or fire, or sumpin'."

"Usually, when it's loose, yeah. But when it's packed in a keg like that, an' you could even open it up and make sure it's packed tight, put a little more in if'n you need to, and it gets hit with a big bullet, the compression will usually make it explode."

"Usually?"

"Well, yeah, usually."

"And if it don't, then what?"

"Well, you get any kind o' fire goin' around that wagon, it will explode sooner or later."

Reuben shook his head, glanced at McDonald. "Well, it beats any plan I could come up with. I'll do it."

"Good, take what you need, just don't take a lamp in

there." McDonald glanced up at the golden colors of the sunset, back at Reuben, "Come on, I'll help you 'fore it gets dark."

With the keg of powder hefted to his shoulder, Reuben walked beside McDonald back to the barn. Reuben asked, "You're sure this will be enough?"

McDonald chuckled. "That's enough to turn that wagon into nothin' but splinters, but when it ignites the other ammunition and such, there won't even be splinters left!" McDonald carried a coil of fuse and when Reuben sat the keg down, he handed off the fuse to the younger man. "That's only as a back-up. Your safest bet is a long shot from behind cover."

Reuben nodded, placing the powder and fuse with the rest of his gear, and with a glance to McDonald, "I'll be headin' out prob'ly 'fore first light." He offered his hand, "Thanks for your help."

"You just do your best to keep those rifles outta the hands o' them Sioux! That's the best thanks you could give me." He paused, looked at the fading colors in the western sky and back to Reuben, "If you're ever back this way..."

"I'll be sure to stop," finished Reuben, shaking McDonald's hand again. The men nodded to one another and turned away, Reuben to his blankets, McDonald to his store and home.

The half-moon was sitting high off Reuben's left shoulder, the lanterns of the night sky were sending their blinking signals to one another, and the clouds had been tucked away for the night. Two lonesome coyotes were lifting their messages high above the tree lined riverbank, and bullfrogs were tuning up to impress their girlfriends. Diamonds in the rough flirted with the lonesome rider, bouncing the lights of the heavens off the ripples of the muddy river as he nudged the animals quietly through the waters. Once on shore, the quiet shuffle of the roan and the mule whispered through the spring grasses on the north side of the Platte. Reuben basked in the solitary time with a glance to the stars to guess the hour to be nearing four in the morning.

He would be well on his way on the Mormon trail side of the river when the sun made its first appearance of the day, yet he could already tell the difference in the terrain. Rolling hills cast dimpled shadows on his right, with juniper, cedar and occasional yucca and patches of prickly pear. The river lay at the edge of the grassland, about a mile and a half away from the hills, but Reuben chose to avoid the main trail and keep to the shadows of the hills. This was Sioux country, and he was a stranger, and interloper, and he rode wary, wanting to get as far as possible before full daylight.

A shadow crossed his trail, and he lifted his eyes to see the wide-spread wings of a golden eagle, recognizable by his shape and size, for the only light was behind him, casting his image in black against the starlit sky. Reuben chuckled, "Mornin' Mr. Eagle, may you have good huntin' this night, but don't forget, we're too big for you, might wanna keep a sharp eye for some o' them long eared jackrabbits! They're more your size!" It was a common practice of lonely travelers to talk to their animals and others that showed themselves. The only companions being those that were here long before him, Reuben appreciated the handiwork of the Creator and often expressed his thanks.

He had no sooner spoken quietly to the eagle than the master of the night tucked his wings and started his dive toward a quarry. Reuben stood in his stirrups just in time to see the golden bird bury its talons in the fur of a rabbit, swooping it off the ground, kicking and muttering its death squeal as it was lifted into the night. It was a rare sight to witness, but it told the eternal story of nature and Reuben knew that rabbit would probably feed hungry new hatchlings in a branch nest somewhere high above the plains. For a moment, all was silent, whether out of fear from the eagle, or respect for the sacrifice, but life continued; coyotes cried again, nighthawks screamed, bullfrogs croaked, and the world turned.

McDonald had given Reuben a detailed description of the terrain and the trail. "The river bears to the west northwest, then 'bout halfway to the Birdwood creek, it turns almost due west. Then 'bout eight or ten miles further, the river kind o' cozies up to them hills and the Birdwood splits 'em and joins up with the Platte. If'n the Sioux are near, maybe even camped some'eres, it'll be up that crick a ways."

"You think they'd be willin' to do some tradin'?" asked Reuben.

"You got anythin' to trade?"

"I picked up some stuff 'fore I left Kearny, beads, gewgaws, knives, needles, stuff like that."

"Well, it might be hard to make it known you was wantin' to trade, but mebbe if you make a camp some'eres they could see you, lay out a blanket with your stuff showin', maybe pitch a fire and show smoke, they might come lookin'. But they might just come raidin', take your stuff, lift your hair, an' leave your naked, muti-lated body bloatin' in the sun!"

"You're a *bundle* of encouragement!" replied Reuben.

"Just speakin' the truth, youngster. You gotta be ready for just 'bout anything when you're dealin' with the natives."

Reuben shook his head at the thought, grinning at the comment of the man, but he also knew he was indeed speaking the truth. Yet he hoped to trade, perhaps not with the Sioux, the way they were on the prowl, but hopefully soon. He was wanting to get a good set of buckskins so he could shed the uniform pants and more. He was tired of always explaining about his time in the war and hoped to distance himself from that time of his life.

The first light of morning began stretching the shadows before him, the trees along the riverbank stood as murmuring shadows, their tall trunks and branches rubbing and creaking in the morning breeze. Clusters of brush in the flats hid the hollows that harbored rabbits, prairie dogs, mice and more in their elongated silhouettes. On the trail for close to five hours, Reuben nudged Blue toward a cluster of junipers that sat at the flank of the hills for it was time for the animals to rest and graze while he fixed a pot of coffee and prepared to partake of the biscuits and bacon provided by Margarite McDonald.

He shielded his hat sized fire under the branches of the juniper, quickly brewed his coffee and sat back to enjoy his repast. This was one of his favorite times of the day when the eastern sky takes on its garments of color; crimson, gold, and orange, to herald the coming of a new day. He took in the glow of color as it painted the east facing slopes and trees, but quickly faded, yielding to the golden orb that peeked over the low horizon, smiling as it bent golden lances of light across the prairie. He had loosened the girths on the animals, tethered them within the grove of junipers but on some fresh spring grasses. He slipped the binoculars from the saddle bags, put his Henry under his arm and started up the slope of the butte behind him. This would be his first look around in the land of the Oglala and he was anxious to gain a better perspective on the land.

It was a gentle slope covered with sage, greasewood, prickly pear cactus and scattered cedar and juniper. As he crested the low butte, he turned to see he was about a hundred feet above the floor of the wide flats that sided the river. He grinned as he found a seat on a wide slab of sandstone and lifted the binoculars for his scan.

———

MAJOR PENDERGRAST STOOD BEFORE THE PEOPLE OF THE wagons, "I'm telling you we don't even know who that man was, and we cannot take his word for anything!"

"But, Major, he saved the women from that Bull fella!" complained one of the men.

"Well, maybe. But what does that have to do with his accusation about rifles? Now, I've spoken with Mr. Newberry, and he assures me he and his wife are bound for Oregon territory to put in a hardware store, providing farm implements for the settlers, and yes, he has some rifles but only because the settlers need modern weapons also! Have you ever been in a general store or trading post that didn't have rifles?" he looked around at the people, saw them looking to one another and talking among themselves. "See there! That's what I mean. Because this stranger came among us and made this wild accusation against a man and his wife that only want to start their business to help the settlers in the area. There's absolutely nothing wrong with that." He glanced from one to the other again, nodding his head and added, "Now, let's get the teams hitched up and get on our way, we still have a long way to go."

The major glanced to the captain, gave a slight nod and the captain went to the Hampton wagon to ask, "Mr. Hampton, I've seen you and your boys ridin' alongside the wagons and doin' a little huntin'. Would it be alright if your boys kinda took the place of the men that were killed? You know, just do a little scoutin' on the flanks of the wagons, maybe take a deer ever now an' then."

Fredrick Hampton looked at the captain, glanced to his boys and saw their eager faces, then to their mother who looked away. The boys, Asa, fifteen, and Abner, thirteen, had taken after their father. Both were full grown, their youth showing only with the peach fuzz on their chin and the mischief in their eyes. The older boy was slightly taller, nearing six foot, lean of frame but showed an unusual confidence, while the younger boy, maybe a couple inches shorter than his brother, was broader shouldered and already showing a muscular build. Both had been hunting with their father for several years, had worked in the fields with him and worked with horses most of their lives. Hampton turned toward the captain. "We can let them try it for a day or two, then talk again."

"Good, good. I'm sure they'll do fine, just fine." He motioned to the boys who stood by their already saddled horses. "Come on, boys, let me show you what we need. You got your rifles?"

The young men eagerly nodded and followed the captain, leading their mounts, anxious to step into the responsibility of a man and scout for the wagons. It was something they had talked about since the start of the trek and now that it was coming to pass, the boys were confident they could fill the shoes of the men that were killed by the stranger.

R euben was belly down on the big rock; binoculars lifted as he scanned the terrain behind the knob. The sun had lifted high in the late morning sky and warmed his back. Long rolling hills seemed to stretch forever, tall grasses waving in the breeze, most a neutral color showing stands from the previous year with green shoots nibbling at their flanks. The entire terrain was like a patchwork quilt with clusters of juniper, cedar and random glades of cottonwood and willow. Low dimples and shades of darker colors showed sage, greasewood, berry bushes and cacti scattered randomly as if the Creator stood high above and cast handfuls of seeds and seedling to sprout across the prairie. Yet it was those patches, differing colors that marked wetlands and waterholes, necessary for the long treks across dry country.

He turned about, looking to the flatlands between the hills and the river. The Platte had the reputation of being too thick to drink and too thin to plow, making fresh water more precious and sought after. Reuben had heard the many stories of entire trains being hit with plagues of cholera as they traveled, leaving bodies and fouled water in their wake. He searched for any sign of Indians: smoke, villages, hunting or raiding parties, but there was nothing.

He looked with naked eye for the first scan, then lifted the field glasses to search more closely the flats between the edge of the hills and the river that twisted lazily through the grassland about a mile or more from the rising hills. Although it was nearing mid-day, a time when most animals had taken shelter from the warm sun and preferred to sleep through the heat, he saw a small herd of pronghorn grazing near the tree line by the river. He started to move his field glasses upstream, but movement caught his eye and he swung back to look at the herd, one had stumbled and fallen, the others instantly took flight choosing an almost direct line toward Reuben's promontory. He focused on the downed animal, waiting a moment or two until a man came from the trees, a native that he guessed to be an Oglala.

The man gave a furtive scan of the flats, then walked toward his kill, dropped to one knee beside it and began the task of dressing the animal. Three more came from the trees and joined the first man in his efforts, one standing watch. Within moments the antelope was dressed out, skinned, boned and the meat bundled nicely in the hide, tied in such a way it made a pack with a strap shouldered by the hunter as the four men returned to the trees. Reuben frowned, wondering about the hunters, were they hunting for meat, or laying in wait for wagons? The trees were thick and gave ample cover for the men, preventing Reuben from seeing how many or what type of camp they had that might give him a better idea what they planned.

The thick cottonwoods, sycamore, willows and more

appeared impenetrable, standing so close that daylight struggled to penetrate the thicket where the native hunters had disappeared. Reuben looked to the west along the flanks of the hills, knowing the Birdwood creek that was his objective was still at least a half-day's ride. Yet he was certain the band of natives, who he presumed were Oglala Sioux, were up to no good. But to stay nearby just in case, could put him at a greater disadvantage in formulating a plan to keep the rifles from the restive Sioux. If there were only the four he saw, they would not be too big a threat, not to wagon trains with thirty to fifty armed men. He kept his eyes on the thicket a few moments longer, thinking, deciding, and rose to his knees beside a gnarly cedar, gathered his gear and descended the hill.

As he readied Blue and Jack, he would need to stay in the hills, keeping under cover of the thicker juniper and cedar until he was well away from the band by the river. It would be slower going, but necessary. He swung aboard the blue, grabbed the lead on Jack and started up the draw between the hills, taking to the trees and picking his trail through the thick grasses. A glance to the sun told him it was midday, and he stripped off his coat, tying it behind the cantle. He loosened the drawstring at his neck, pulling wide the loose collars and seeking relief from the hot sun from the slight breeze on his sweaty chest and neck.

He knew the wagons on the Mormon trail would be moving out sometime earlier today and would undoubtedly make good time, seasoned travelers that they were; at least the handlers of the wagons. Those men had come from the promised land of the Latter-Day Saints to gather the last of the faithful and had already traveled this trail twice before. Although many of the wagons were drawn by Oxen, they were steady and proven and would use every bit of daylight to make as many miles as possible, usually rivaling and even bettering the miles of trains drawn by mules and horses. Reuben found it easy to convince himself the larger train would be in no trouble with the small band of hunters he saw in the woods by the river.

———

STRIPS OF MEAT HUNG FROM WILLOW WITHES OVER THE licking flames, dripping their juices into the fire, snapping, and sizzling, taunting the hungry warriors. Five men sat around the small fire, that burned low underneath the wide branches of an old oak, thick leaves dissipating the smoke and smells of the cooking meat. Kicking Bear was the self-appointed leader of the small band, chosen from those that were closest to him and proven in battle, even though all were young and eager. Kicking Bear said, "The white man, Captain Yeager, expects us to pay for the rifles with gold coin, but I have a better plan." He paused as he looked from one to the other of the men. "We will take women from the trains, trade them for the rifles, keep the gold for more rifles later."

"He will do this? When these are not his women?" asked Eagle Thunder.

"White men are fools! They will do anything for their women!"

"I want a woman!" grumbled the youngest one of the bunch, Walking Elk.

The others laughed at the somber faced young man, even though he stood taller than all of them, as he voiced his most common complaint. They knew he had tried to court several young women, offered good bride prices, but none wanted him, choosing to convince their fathers to wait for another. He had become the butt of many jokes and much laughter, making him angry and reticent, yet determined to prove himself as a great warrior.

Flying Hawk looked at his brother. "You have scouted the wagons, what is your plan?"

Kicking Bear scooted closer to the others. "The women of these wagons wash themselves and their things apart from the men. When they stop at the Birdwood creek, we will take them. Each one will take one," he held up a stiff finger before each man as he scowled. "One!" Each man nodded in return, until Kicking Bear continued, "We will take them to our camp to wait for the rifles. The captain is to come in the night, soon. I believe it is their wagons that follow those with the women."

"The white men will follow their women," growled Black Fox, the youngest of the three brothers and the one named after his father.

"We will have our other warriors waiting when the men come," stated Kicking Bear, looking at the others with a smug expression as if he had settled all doubts. He reached for a strip of meat, prompting the others to do the same, eating as they thought about the coming challenges.

Walking Elk was focused on his eating, but deep in thought. He considered what Kicking Bear had said and planned, but he mentally reviewed the trail of the wagons that followed the north side of the river, picturing every possible site that might give an opportunity to stealthily sneak into the wagons and steal a woman. Kicking Bear's plan was to strike at a creek crossing when the women were separated, but what about other times when the women went into the woods to gather berries or more? Other wagons had stopped near here, why not the one with the women? Walking Elk grinned at the thought, chewing his meat, and ignoring the others, but Kicking Bear was watching him, knowing his cousin was determined to get himself a woman, not one to trade for guns. Kicking Bear knew the way his cousin thought, that if he could not court a woman of their village, he could steal a woman from the white men and make her his own.

Kicking Bear walked to where Walking Elk had stretched out on the grass, resting on one elbow as he watched the others. Bear sat beside him. "Are you thinking of trying for a woman?"

Elk frowned at his friend, slowly shaking his head. "I want a woman of my own. Not one to trade for rifles. If I can take one from the wagons, one that I want, then I will do so."

"There are many men with rifles," suggested Kicking Bear.

"Then I will take a woman and a rifle!" declared Walking Elk.

"If you take a woman, and it ruins our plans for rifles, then what?"

"I must have a woman." He scowled at Kicking Bear. "You have a woman," and nodded to the others, "They have women." He looked back at Bear, "I do not have a woman."

Kicking Bear was silent a moment, looking at his friend, thinking. He lifted his eyes to the man. "I scouted these wagons two days, some women go by themselves into the woods. It might be that when they come near here, they would do the same."

Walking Elk sat up, eagerness showing on his face.

"That is what I thought they would do, and I could take one," he paused, looked at the ground and mumbled, "if she is suitable for me."

Kicking Bear grinned. "We will wait for the wagons, see where they stop, then decide."

Walking Elk stood, grinning. "It is good!" he declared and trotted to the edge of the trees, anxious for a sighting of the wagons and the women. Elk was a big man standing several inches over six feet, broad shoulders that were of greater span than an axe handle, yet with a heavy forehead, lantern jaw, and broad nose, his head was the most captivating feature of the man. Piercing eyes told of an intelligence that his visage denied, but the fire behind them also warned of a viciousness that was kindled by an evil bent that delighted in inflicting pain and death, the very traits that made him a great warrior. Although the others often belittled him, they knew the limits of his patience and having seen the result of his vengeance, they were careful with their jibes. It was little wonder that the women of the village avoided the man.

D usk was lowering its curtain when Reuben chose a camp in the winding draw that twisted between a pair of buttes. The draw fed the narrow valley of the Birdwood creek and offered him a good promontory to view both the valley and the flats with the North Platte river.

The mouth of the Birdwood creek held a cut back valley, green with new growth and lying out of sight from the flatlands of the Platte. For about five miles the valley spread on both sides of the meandering creek, the thirsty grassland soaking up the moisture carried by the little stream. From Reuben's promontory, he scanned the fertile valley, spotted several deer, a small herd of antelope, a lone bull bison, and several coyotes, but nothing else of significance.

Beside the stream, a grassy flat showed sign of being used as a camp, the remains of a cookfire, grazed down grass, horse apples, and what appeared to be sites for bedrolls. He focused in on the camp, searched the valley floor for a trail and spotted a well-used trail that hugged the base of the hills and disappeared in the upper reaches of the wide valley. Reuben took his time, wanting to learn every facet of the wider valley, possible meeting places for the gun runners and natives, as well as potential ambush points. With each possibility, he also looked for high ground for him to use to oversee the huddle.

A quick glance showed the fading of dusk and the deepening of darkness. The rest of his scout would have to be done after first light, but there was still a day or more before the wagon train would near the confluence of the Birdwood and North Platte. He crabbed back from the crest of the hill, came to a crouch, and returned to his camp.

The animals were grazing lazily on the grassy clearing beside the trickle of spring water, Blue lifted his head as Reuben neared and satisfied, dropped his nose to the spring sprouts. The draw was well hidden, making an 'S' curve from its mouth at the valley before reaching the little spring that was well hidden in a shoulder of rock and covered by cedar. With a cluster of junipers at the base of the hill, Reuben built a hat-sized fire to make his coffee and sear the last of his fresh meat. He had thought about taking one of the deer he saw earlier but did not want to risk his rifle shot being heard and giving away his presence. Besides, he had a bag of jerked meat in the panniers and some dried apples and peaches he still carried from Kearny.

REUBEN CHECKED THE TIME BY THE STARS, GUESSING IT TO be close to four in the morning. The stars were still telegraphing their presence with brilliant blinkers, the moon was lowering in the west and the night sky was clear. He checked the tether for the mule, allowing for ample room to graze and to reach water without showing himself, tightened the girth on his saddle atop Blue and stepped aboard. With a bit of a nudge with his knees, the big blue roan took to the hills, bound to the north to wend their way through the sandhills and go further upstream on the Birdwood. After passing a round-top butte, he pointed the roan toward the valley.

They had been paralleling the stream and soon broke from the hills to follow a sandy bed dry creek into the bunch grass valley. From his promontory the previous day, he spotted what he thought was a well-used trail that sided the stream and continued north into the sandhills, it was that trail he wanted to examine. The low rolling hills surrendered their claim to high ground and the flats showed sage, greasewood, and scattered bunch grass mixed with cacti. Reuben pushed into the open, making his way by fading moonlight nearer the creek, always watching for the trail. He was on it before he realized, reined up and dropped to the ground for a close-up look at the recent sign on the trail. Many horses had traveled south, a few north most recently. He stood, looking up and down the trail. Even in the dim light of early morning, he could see the valley narrow to the north, and he caught a whiff of wood smoke.

Blue nudged him and he stroked the big roan's neck and head, but when the horse was insistent, he mounted up and pointed him back up the sandy bottomed draw. It would not do to be found alone in the middle of Sioux country and he did not hanker to make his presence known before the problem of the rifles was settled.

When the pale grey chased the darkness from the sky, Reuben had mounted the highest knoll in the area, wanting a better look at the lay of the land and maybe find where the smell of smoke emanated. He had learned from the war to make any reconnoiter before the first full light of day. It is in those early hours when most are at their drowsiest and least attentive. He could only assume human nature was the same whether with the Confederates or the natives; nature is nature.

Thin wisps of smoke spiraled into the morning light to reveal the location of the Oglala village. Still about a mile away and probably nigh unto ten miles from the mouth of the valley and the confluence with the Platte, the village was nestled in the valley at the forks of the Birdwood. Most of the lodges were on the east side of the creek in the wide nook of the confluence, probably formed eons ago by spring flood waters carving their way to the distant Platte.

From where he lay belly down, he guessed there to be fifty or sixty lodges, and perhaps more were obscured by the hillsides and the fork of the creeks. But the way he understood it, for every lodge there would be at least two warriors, so that would mean at least a hundred warriors and probably half again as many. More than enough to take any wagon train if a hundred or more were armed with Springfield rifles. He slowly shook his head as he considered the potential slaughter that would mean for the many wagon trains still moving west. With one last scan of the village and the valley, he slid back from the knob and returned to Blue.

Taking a different route back to the camp, he used the sandy bottomed draws, bunch grass flats, and more to make his trail less obvious and more difficult to follow. As he rode, he again contemplated his possible actions. Although he had already chosen several spots to use for his ambush, nothing could be certain until the wagons came and the man with the big Conestoga separated from the others. But for now, he was hungry, tired, and more concerned with his own comforts and his animals.

———

ABNER PUSHED THE CARCASS OF THE DOE OFF THE RUMP OF his horse, smiling broadly as he said, "That's for you and your family, Mrs. Betts," as he smiled at her daughter, Madeline. "Me'n Asa were outriders today, an' we each got a deer so I thought you folks might could use this'n."

"Why thank you, Abner. That's awful nice of you," she glanced from the young man to her daughter, "Isn't it, Maddy?"

The girl smiled, nodding to Abner, "Yes Ma, it is nice of Abner to think of us."

"Aw, shucks, ain't nuthin', just a little ol' doe. But Ma says they're good eatin'," he added, eager to please. He had doffed his hat and now jammed it back on, "Reckon I better be gettin' back. Ma's gettin' supper ready fer us and we been ridin' all day, so we're mighty hungry and tired too." He puffed up his chest and twisted around a bit, reining his horse around. He waved to Maddy and nudged his horse away as he heard her, "Bye, Abner. Thank you!"

"THE CAP'N ALSO RECRUITED MALACHI BECKER FOR AN outrider; put him on the left side, me'n Abner on the right side near the river. We both got a deer outta the same bunch as they was comin' to water," explained Asa, the older of the two brothers, as he spoke to his father.

"So, you enjoyed the riding today?" asked his father.

"Yeah, nuthin' to it. The cap'n said it was mainly to

bag some meat and keep an eye out for any danger, you know, Indians an' such."

"Indians?!" asked his mother, alarm showing in her eyes.

"There weren't any Indians, Eliza. They just had to watch out for any, bring the warning to the captain and the wagons. They don't hafta fight 'em."

"Are you sure?" asked the fearful mother, wiping her hands in her apron as she looked at her two boys.

"They're in no more danger riding out there than they would be driving the wagon. They're smart young men and it's time they shouldered a little responsibility. Time to grow up!" declared Fredrick, his pride in his boys showing.

As the family was readying for their supper, the captain walked up to their wagon, came close to the boys. "You men did fine today, just like I thought you would. Keep it up and by the time we get to Fort Laramie, you can handle just about anything." He looked from one to the other, then to their father. "You have some young men to be proud of, Mr. Hampton." He looked at the brothers again. "Tomorrow I'd like you, Abner, to take point. Asa, you take the left flank an' Malachi will take the right. Abner, you'll need to stay a couple miles out front, and you'll need to be extra watchful. Don't be concerned about takin' any game, just scout the trail for us. Any danger or problem, you shinny on back and let us know, got that?"

"Yessir, I've got it."

"Good, good." He glanced to Fredrick and Eliza, back to the boys. "Evenin' then. Get some good rest, men, need to be on your toes tomorrow!" and waved over his shoulder as he left.

Asa leaned over to his brother, "Hear that, Abner, he called us men!"

Abner chuckled. "That's cuz we are, Asa, we are!"

It was by the grey light of morning that the wagons made their way past the two-story log stage station/trading post also known as McDonald's Ranch. Smoke was curling from the chimney, a stage stood beside the corrals, and the hostler was busy with harnessing the mules. The station stood about a hundred yards south of the wagon trail, the Overland trail forking from the Platte River Road and following the South Platte. The wagon trail bent to the river for the crossing of the south fork, with the North Platte bending to the northwest.

The lead wagon was the Hightower wagon, driven by Hiram with his wife Hannah on the spring seat beside him. Their nine-year-old twin girls, Dorcas, and Dinah, standing in the box behind their parents, excited about their first river crossing. When the captain waved him on, Hiram slapped the leads on the rumps of his mules, and they stepped into the slow moving and shallow water. The gravel bottom crossing was easy going, the water barely knee-deep on the mules, and the wagon made the crossing without any difficulty. Within just less than an hour, the entire train had made the crossing and were stretched out on the trail beside the North Platte.

"So, Captain, how far to Fort Laramie?" asked Hiram, proud of making the river crossing and feeling he could master just about any difficulty, even distance.

The big man, Otis Yeager, or captain, grinned and chuckled, "Oh, 'bout three weeks or so, dependin'."

"Dependin'? Dependin' on what, Captain?"

"Just about anything and everything, you never know

out here in the west. Most anything you see will kick you, bite you, sting you, eat you, or kill you. And if they don't, the Indians will. And they'll strip you, cut you, scalp you, and leave your body to bloat in the sun. And if the bugs and animals don't get you, and the Indians don't get you, the lightnin' storms, tornadoes, flash floods, mudslides and rockslides will. So, like I said, it depends on which one gets you first!" The captain chuckled, kneed his horse past the wagon and waved over his shoulder at the family driving the first wagon. Hiram Hightower shook his head, glanced at his wife just as she said, "And if they don't get'chu, I will!" and slapped his shoulder, laughing and shaking her head to look at the girls standing and smiling behind their daddy. They were used to their parents cajoling with one another and were glad to join in the fun.

And they were two days away from the confluence of the Birdwood creek and the North Platte river where the gun runners and the Sioux warriors were to meet up and make their deal for the rifles, maybe.

The ponderous oxen trudged along the dusty trail, every step seeming to be at great effort, but they never faltered. The drawn wagons, wheels lifting clouds of dust with each turn, axles squealing, wagon boxes and hardware steadily creaking and groaning protesting with each mile, yet they continued. Captain Stenhouse had passed the word they would cross the Birdwood Creek and make camp along the bank beyond the sharp bend before the confluence with the Platte. "There's plenty fresh water, womenfolk'll be able to do the washin' an' such. We'll fill our water barrels. Might be some time 'fore we find fresh water the like o' this."

Reuben had crossed the creek, moving his camp into the sandhills nearer the Platte with better access to the valley of the Birdwood and a promontory atop a knoll that stood about a hundred feet above the valley floor. He was amidst a cluster of bunch grass as he moved his field glasses to take in the arriving train. While the wagons began forming up to their rectangular camp, all wagons facing west, those on the north and south edges of their formation were end-to-end, while those on the west and east, were side by side. The animals were taken to water, then turned into the middle of the square. It was a tight formation and one that, if need be, could be easily defended.

The people worked in concert, each to his or her assigned task and Reuben marveled at the efficiency of the company. Cookfires were soon blazing, pots hanging above the flames, women busy with the meal preparations, while men tended the animals and the gear. Reuben saw a group of women walking to the low bank of the creek, arms full of clothing, apparently bound for laundry duties. Another smaller group started from the wagons, bound for the trees and brush, each carrying a container of sorts, baskets, bags, and more, probably looking for berries although there would be few ripe at this time of year, but wild onions, and other edibles were to be found.

A glance behind him to the west showed the sun was about to turn in for the day, settling on the western horizon and beginning to paint the sky with its farewell colors. The trail often called the Mormon trail because so many of the faithful had traveled the north bank route, improving the trail as they passed, making the way for those that would follow all the better, was now on the isthmus of land that lay between the Birdwood and the North Platte. The camp was on the northern edge near the smaller creek and thick woods stood between the camp and the bigger river, woods that held a great variety of hardwoods and berry bushes. It was into these woods that the younger women of the train ventured in search of early season berries and any other edibles they could find. It had become their assigned task to gather what plants and berries they could, while the older women tended to the meal preparations.

Reuben had watched the small group of young women go into the trees but focused his attention on the work of the men, concerned about their precautions about a possible Indian attack. He remembered McDonald expressing his exasperation with the leader of the train and his lack of concern about the safety of his people as regards the dangers of the restive Sioux. "I swear that man makes my blood boil! Just cuz he's been this way before and didn't have any trouble with the Sioux, he thinks they won't have any trouble this time! And even if they do, he said his men and their rifles would make any attackers turn tail an' run!" McDonald was fuming and stomping around, knowing he was helpless to intervene with the Mormon wagon train, and continued his rant, "It's idjits like that what makes it bad fer ever'one else!"

Reuben chuckled at the memory as he scanned the camp of the wagon train. The brilliant colors of the sunset had faded, the curtain of dusk was lowering, and he lowered the glasses, looked at the twinkling cookfires already casting shadowy waifs about the camp. He started to rise when a shout came from below and people jumped and ran to the edge of the formation. One young woman was running from the trees, screaming, and pointing but she was too far away for Reuben to make out what was being said, her alarm speaking for her as others ran to her side. The gestures, shouts, and gathering of men told much as one man began to bark orders, sending men back to the wagons for weapons and more. The light was fading fast and whatever had happened had to be discovered and resolved quickly for when darkness fell, hope dimmed.

———

"Isaiah, you and three men, get your rifles and lanterns. Go directly south from the far corner of the wagons, search until you reach the river. If no luck, move west a bit, come back north." Captain Stenhouse looked at other men nearby, picking another. "Edmund, you do the same, three men, weapons and lanterns, but start directly south from the southwest corner, go to the river and back."

Another man stepped forward. "Captain?"

"MacArthur, you do the same, but start from right here," as he turned to point toward the tree line, "and go into the trees, there! You'll need to strike due south to the river, come back east to meet Edmund Bunker, and come back to the wagons. When you return, if you don't have the women, stay with the wagons, get Bunker an' Isaiah Chislett to stay with their men also. Go!" he demanded, motioning the man to the wagons.

He turned to see four other men waiting. "Go, get your weapons and lanterns, return here. We'll take the west edge, now git!"

Reuben turned his attention from the wagons, lifting his field glasses to scan the trees. Although the shadows and darkness had shrouded the woods, he hoped to see movement of some kind, anything to tell of what had alarmed the men of the wagons. He moved the glasses side to side, then movement at the far edge caught his attention. The wide ribbon of the Platte showed silver in the beginning of moonlight, several riders were splashing across the waters. Within moments, they disappeared into the trees on the far side of the river, the rapidly fading light and dimpled terrain, pocked with juniper, cedar, and sage, gave a camouflage that Reuben could not penetrate. But the fleeing warriors, easily identified by their skimpy attire, lances and war shields, and the way they sat their horses, were undoubtedly the cause of the alarm. He was not certain, but the glimpse of the riders gave Reuben the impression the horses were riding double, maybe with captives.

Reuben sat back on his haunches, the field glasses in his lap, as he set his mind to work. What would he be doing if he were the Oglala? Why take the captives when the rifles are on their way? He turned to the side, looking to the valley of the Birdwood, the moon was waxing to full, but was little more than half. Yet the clear night, the sky showing the lanterns of the stars shining brightly, and the quiet air gave Reuben a good view of the valley floor. As he waited, he pondered, trying to consider all angles and possibilities, but as he bided his time, he saw no other movement, yet he also knew skilled warriors such as the Sioux could easily evade detection, especially in their own back yard.

Reuben strode down the back side of the knoll, went to Blue and tightened the girth, stepped aboard, and reined the roan around to go to the wagons. He pointed Blue to the northwest corner of the wagon formation and as he neared, he called out, "Helloo the camp!"

and stopped, waiting for a response. He saw a shadowy figure step between the wagons, holding a rifle across his chest. "Who're you and what do you want?" called the man.

"I'm a friend and I'd like to talk to your captain!"

"What about?"

"About the little ruckus you've got goin' on."

"What do you know about it?"

Reuben shook his head, nudged Blue forward. "Let me come in and we'll talk." He saw another man step beside the first, speak in low tones and the first man responded, "Come ahead on, but keep your hands empty!"

Reuben had lifted his free hand shoulder high, nodded to the man and gigged Blue to the break between the wagons. The roan stepped over the lowered tongue, crowding the two men back and Reuben brought him to a stop, looked at the two men. "Alright if I get down?"

"Yeah, but easy."

Reuben shook his head but was understanding of the heightened concern of the men. He looked at the first man, a middle-aged, well set-up man who held one of the new Spencer repeater rifles. "I'd like to talk to your captain, Stenhouse, isn't it?"

"How come you know Captain Stenhouse?"

"Saw him back at McDonalds, the stage stop."

The man slowly lifted his head to acknowledge the stop, motioned with his rifle for Reuben to walk before him. "The Cap'ns over yonder by that fire in the middle there."

As the three men neared the fire, others turned to see them, one man stepping forward, "Who do we have here?"

"Cap'n, this fella just rode in here, says he wants to talk to you 'bout what's happenin'."

The captain looked at Reuben, frowning. "What do you know?" he growled.

Reuben answered, "Not much. But I saw you folks gettin' all upset, saw you send your men into the woods. So, what happened?"

"Who are you and why are you here?" demanded the captain, still suspicious of the intruder.

"I'm Reuben Grundy. I'm here because I'm scoutin' for the wagon train that's about a day behind you on the other side of the river. I saw you back at McDonald's. I was up there," he pointed to the knoll, "lookin' things over when your train pulled in here. I was just comin' down when that girl came from the woods screamin'."

"That girl was one of a group of girls gathering berries and such. But she said she was off by herself, heard a commotion, and when she went looking for the others, she saw some Indians and came running back to tell us about it."

"And you didn't find any in the woods."

"No, we didn't."

"That's because I saw several riders go bustin' across the river to the south, into the trees and hills on that side."

"Why didn't you shoot?" asked one of the men near the fire. He stood up and shook his fist, glaring at Reuben, demanding an answer.

Reuben slowly shook his head, "I've made some good shots in my life, but never one of a mile and at a target that could be carryin' some mighty precious cargo."

The captain turned to the others. "Alright, men, you know what to do. We'll meet back here at the fire in fifteen minutes!"

"You're not goin' out tonight, are you?" asked Reuben incredulously.

"We can't leave our young women in the hands of those heathen! There's no telling what they'll do!"

"Uh, Captain, you might want to rethink that a mite."

"And why should we do that?"

"Let's see, you've got what, maybe forty armed men?"

"About that."

"Well, about ten miles up that valley there," nodding to the north and the valley of the Birdwood, "is a Sioux village with at least a hundred fifty warriors. Now, unless I miss my guess, the warriors that took your women, circled around" pointing to the Platte on the south, "and took their captives back to their village. And they'll probably be expectin' you to do somethin' just that foolish as to leave your other women folk and your supplies and young'uns right here with just a handful of men to protect them. It would be just like them to wait until you head out after that handful, and then swoop down on your wagons and leave you nothin' but ashes to return to, that is if there are any of you left alive to return."

The captain looked askance at Reuben, glanced around the group of men and women that were waiting for his direction, and said, "You might be right. But we can't let them take our women!"

"Well, maybe there's another way, but not tonight," responded Reuben, stepping closer to the captain, and moving to the cookfire with the coffee pot he saw dancing on the rocks.

R euben returned to his camp, thinking about the captive girls, the Sioux, and the gun runners with the other wagon train. No matter how he figured it, the result was the same, death and destruction. He was one man, what could he do against an entire village of proven warriors? He was confident in his ability to stealthily approach an enemy camp, even take out some chosen targets and make his escape. He had done it often enough with the Sharpshooters, but the Sioux had been making war for a lot longer than the rebels, and were at home in this wilderness, more so than himself.

It had long been his habit to make informed choices and as things stood now, he was less than informed. He needed to know more about the village, the warriors, and the captives. The only way to do that would be to make a moonlight reconnoiter. He had started derigging Blue but as he thought, he settled the saddle back in place, tightened the girth and swung aboard. As he started from his camp, he glanced to the starlit sky, the rising half-moon, and the milky way stacked in a corner of the vast darkness. He was reminded of one of his mother's favorite scriptures, Psalm 19:1 *The heavens declare the glory of God; and the firmament sheweth His handywork.*

"Well, God, it's easy to see your glory up there, but down here things aren't so great. Now, I'm goin' out to see if I can find those girls the Oglala kidnapped, and I'm hopin', well, I guess I'm prayin', that you'll kinda guide me a mite. You know, get me to the right place at the right time, hopefully 'fore somethin' bad happens to them girls. And, Lord, I know I haven't been doin' too much talkin' to you lately, but I'm fixin' to do better 'bout that. We both remember the time that I prayed and asked Jesus to be my Savior and to grant me that free gift of eternal life like it says in your Bible, and I know I haven't been livin' quite like I should, what with all the killin' and such. But the parson said that was no different than David and Goliath, so I'm countin' on that bein' true. So, Lord, I guess what I'm askin' is for you to work through me to get this done, cuz I shore can't do it by myself! And like my momma said, I ask this in Jesus' name, Amen."

He had cut the trail of the captors, and as he suspected, they had ridden wide around the camp of the wagons and were following the trail that would take them upstream of the Birdwood and eventually to the village. Reuben reined up and stepped down to examine the tracks more closely, his eyes accustomed to the dim light of the moon, but it was easy to see the fresh tracks of six horses, all carrying heavy but not in a hurry. He stood, looking up the trail, wondering what was going on in the minds of the warriors who were either assuming there would be no pursuit, or were hoping there would be and were not in a hurry to leave any pursuers behind. He had known others in the war that were often overconfident and even arrogant to the point of assuming no one would dare to confront them and if they did there would be no contest. Usually that attitude resulted in a sudden realization of their mistake just before they were dispatched to meet their maker.

He swung back aboard and moved closer to the tree line beside the creek, letting Blue pick his way through the grass and undergrowth. When they had traveled about three miles from the mouth of the valley, and about four or five miles from the wagon encampment, Blue was stepping lightly, slowly, head up, ears pricked, and nostrils flaring. Reuben leaned down on the roan's neck, whispered in Blue's ear, "What is it boy, what you smellin'?" He stroked Blue's neck, looking into the shadows, straining to see into the darkness. The moon was stacking shadows upon shadows, the light breeze moving the branches, rubbing one against another as they groaned and creaked like specters in the blackness.

Blue stopped, head high, his ears slowly moving forward and back. Reuben leaned low, and got a whiff of stale smoke, a fire had been doused by water. Reuben stroked the neck of the roan, then slid to the ground, Henry rifle in hand. He dropped the rein to ground tie Blue, searched the trees and brush for a break where he could enter the thicket, and slowly moved into the shadows.

He spotted the clearing, lances of moonlight piercing the tree cover and dimpling the grassy flat with random shadows. He went down to a crouch, hung the Henry at his back with the sling, and went to his belly to snake through the grass. Each movement slow and measured, lightly placing each hand, each knee, ensuring there was nothing underneath to give away his presence. The dew of the night dampened the leaves, silencing their movement as Reuben pushed them aside. Overhead a big owl called his question into the night only to be answered by a bullfrog at creek side. As he neared the clearing, he lifted his head slightly, searching for each warrior and each captive. He had expected to see at least one on watch but could not make out any but the sleeping forms.

Movement beside a gnarly cottonwood caught his attention. He slowly turned his head to see a big man, seated at the tree, who appeared to be dozing. He was the one on watch. Without looking directly at the man, knowing a continual stare can often be felt, he made out another smaller form beside him on the ground. He looked back at the others, saw what he was certain were the captives, apparently bound back-to-back and lying on their sides. Both pair had their feet to what had been the fire, their heads toward the creek. Beyond them, four men were nearer the trees and more difficult to discern their position, but none moved and the sounds of steady breathing, even snoring, came from the shadows.

Reuben cradled his chin on his hands, looking and thinking, but knew he had to act quickly. He snaked backwards into the brush, came to a crouch, and started through the thicket toward the lone sentry. With the cottonwoods between them, Reuben picked his steps, knowing the cast-off branches would snap and give him away, and slowly made his way closer. He could see the broad shoulders of the big man extending on either side of the cottonwood trunk, yet he did not move, and his raspy breathing was regular, steady. Beside him and under his hand and forearm lay one of the women captives, a little restless, occasionally whimpering, but the man had become used to her movement and sound which masked the same from Reuben.

Another step closer and Reuben slipped his razor-sharp Bowie knife from the scabbard at the small of his back. Another step, the whisper of his movement through the grass seeming loud, and the man mumbled and moved. Reuben froze, one foot lifted slightly but he slowly touched his toe to the ground to steady himself, his breathing gone shallow, the blade glimmering in the moonlight. Another moment, the man settled, his breathing became rhythmic and steady. Reuben moved another step closer, now within reach of the cotton-wood, it would be a stretch to reach around one side, use the knife on the other, but...his left hand lifted as he pushed his chest and cheek against the rough bark, took a deep breath and wrapped his arm around the trunk, covered the man's mouth, gripped his jaw, and jerked it to the side. The Bowie flashed in the moonlight, the blade against the man's throat and a quick slice as the blade cut through his throat, severing his windpipe, and almost decapitating the man. He kicked out, gurgled, grabbing at the hand on his face, kicked again and lay still. Reuben looked at the others, one man rolled to his side, a horse snorted and shifted his feet, the girl beside the big man rolled from under his arm and stared at the gaping throat, the wide eyes that stared into the dark-ness, and started to scream, but Reuben lunged at her, his hand over her mouth and hissed in her ear, "I'm here to help you! Quiet!"

She looked wide-eyed at Reuben, recognizing him only as a white man, and nodded. Reuben slowly lowered his hand, "Can you shoot a rifle?" he whispered.

The girl eagerly nodded, glancing from Reuben to the sleeping warriors. Reuben slipped the rifle from his back, handed it to the girl and whispered instructions to which the girl nodded and with a quick glance to the dead man, she stood beside Reuben. He motioned to her to watch the others while he freed the girls. "Shoot if you have to!" Again, she nodded, pointing to the girls with her chin as she stood feet apart, rifle held pointed at the warriors.

Reuben went to the first pair, put a hand over the first girl's mouth and as she came awake, eyes wide and fearful, he whispered, "I will cut you loose, then you free the others." He quickly cut the bonds at her feet, her hands and between the two. She slowly sat up, rubbing her wrists, accepted the knife and whispered into her friend's ear, and began cutting her free.

Reuben stood, slipped his pistol from the holster, and watched the warriors. He had no sooner stood than one man rolled to the side, looked at Reuben and quickly sprang to his feet. Reuben hollered, "No!" holding his pistol before him. The others came instantly awake and rose, shouting to one another. One man on the far side, bent to retrieve his weapon, came up with a trade Fusil rifle, and the Henry roared in the girl's hand, bucking, and spitting fire. The slug took the warrior dead center in the chest and before the smoke cleared, the girl had jacked another round into the chamber and swung the muzzle toward the next man.

The second girl was cutting the second pair free, working frantically as the girls stared and one muttered, "Elly! You killed him!"

The girl with the rifle did not take her eyes off the others as she answered, "And I'm ready to shoot them too!" she declared. The warriors spoke among themselves, looking to one another and to the girl with the rifle and Reuben. They lunged together but the Henry barked again, the slug digging dirt at one man's feet and Reuben shot one of the others, the Remington slug penetrating the man's shoulder, spinning him to the side and dropping him to the ground. The third man froze in place, shocked that the rifle in the girl's hand fired again without reloading, and he watched the girl jack another round in the chamber, confused by her action, but not daring another charge.

The two warriors stood until Reuben motioned one to tend to his wounded friend while the other remained standing. Reuben looked at the four girls, now standing to the side watching both the warriors and Reuben and their companion, Elly. Reuben said, "Girls, if you can, fetch those horses so you can ride while Elly and I guard these fellas."

As the four went to the picketed horses, Elly said, "Why don't we just shoot them and be done with it?"

Reuben glanced at her, saw the anger burning in her eyes, slowly shook his head. "Uh, these boys have about a hundred or more friends just a little ways up this valley. I don't think you want to make things worse on your folks back at the wagons."

The girls had mounted the horses, their skirts bunched around their legs, and handed off the lead to the last horse to Elly. Handing the rifle to Reuben, Elly bellied down on the Indian pony, hopped up and swung a leg over to sit smugly on the horse that had carried her from the wagons. She gave a quick look to the bloody man by the tree, then to the one she shot, and said, "Hand me the rifle and I'll cover you while you fetch your horse."

"No need," said Reuben, but handed off the rifle anyway, and sounded a short whistle toward the trees. The crashing of brush told him Blue was coming and he broke through the trees to come to Reuben's side, nodding his head as if he approved of what he saw, and nudged Reuben with his muzzle. Reuben chuckled, "I'm glad to see you too, Blue." He stepped into the stirrup, swung a leg over and looked down at the three warriors. He used his limited sign language to tell them to go back to their village and stay away from the wagons. He looked at Elly, "You lead out, the wagons are thataway!" nodding downstream.

After they were on their way, Reuben backed Blue from the clearing, reined him around and took off in pursuit of the girls. He soon caught them, motioned them to slow the horses to a walk. "It's still a couple miles to the wagons, don't wanna hafta walk, do ya?"

"Who are you?" asked Elly, moving her horse close to Blue. She was a pretty girl, long blonde hair that Reuben could tell would usually be in long curls but was a little mussed after their ordeal. She had dimples in her light complexion, and from what he could tell in the moonlight, she had everything else that made a girl a woman. He chuckled and answered, "Muh name's Reuben. I was just scoutin' the trail when I came across your wagons, saw a little of what happened, and had to convince your captain not to leave the wagons to go after you girls. Thought the rest of the Oglala might attack the train if they did."

"Does Reuben have a last name?" asked the girl, a pert smile showing.

"That depends."

"Depends, on what?"

"Does Elly have a last name?"

"McGuire, Eleanor Ann McGuire."

"I'm Reuben Grundy. Pleased to meet you, Miss McGuire."

"Really, Reuben. We've killed Indians together, I

think that makes us close enough to be on a first name basis, don't you?"

"Uh, reckon so, Elly. By the way, my rifle please?" he asked, holding his hand toward her.

She looked down at the rifle that lay across her lap, up at Reuben. "Well, if you insist, but I was getting attached to it. I heard about these, and I kinda like the way it works." She smiled up at him as he took the rifle, ducked her head coyly. "Might hafta get me one!" And both knew she was not talking about the rifle.

"Hello, the camp!" hollered Reuben as they neared the darkened wagon formation.

"Yo! Who are you?"

"I'm Reuben, the man that came in earlier, and I've got some women with me!"

"Come on in, keep your hands high!" responded the sentry.

Reuben grinned, nodded to Elly to lead the way, and held back as the women passed. As they entered the wagon formation, the alarm went out and shouts could be heard throughout the wagons. People came running, most in their night clothes, wrapped in a blanket, but determined not to miss the excitement. Reuben sat just inside the formation, leaning on the pommel of his saddle, grinning at the joyous reunions. Mothers hugged their daughters; men hugged their families and Lorenzo Stenhouse walked over to look up at Reuben. "I don't know how you did it, but we are forever grateful."

"We were lucky. I thought sure they'd go back to their village, but they camped upstream a few miles and I was able to sneak up on 'em, but the women helped." He nodded to the excited throng. "You've got some mighty strong women there; they'll make some of your men fine wives."

Stenhouse followed Reuben's gaze, noted he was looking at the McGuire girl, and explained, "Our women learn to be strong from an early age. Our families have known persecution for years, which is why so many of us have made the journey to the promised land." He looked up at Reuben. "What about you, Reuben? Do you have a family?"

Reuben looked down at the captain of the train. "No, Mr. Stenhouse, my family was murdered by some charlatans posin' as Home Guard. All I have left is my sister, who is married to a fine man, a businessman, and is raisin' a family." He lifted his eyes to the distant stars that glimmered above the western horizon. "My home is somewhere out here in the west and is yet to be found." He looked down at Stenhouse. "Uh, I'm sure it need not be said, but you might want to get your wagons on the trail at first light. We killed a couple Oglala, left the others afoot, and they'll be goin' to their village. That probably means they'll be returnin' for a little retaliation, blood vengeance, so it might be best if you're long gone."

"That was our original plan, until the women were taken, but with all this excitement, we might get under way even earlier. I'm sure the ladies will fix a fine breakfast if you're interested in sharing our table?"

Reuben grinned. "A good meal is something I seldom say no to," as he swung his leg over the roan and stepped down.

"You wait here, I would like to let the ladies know we'll have company for breakfast," responded the captain, a slight grin tugging at the corner of his mouth as he looked from Reuben to the McGuire family, all of whom were looking their way.

He soon returned, grinning at Reuben. "The McGuire family said if I let you get away without coercing you to stay for breakfast, they would, or at least the ladies would, tan my hide. Now, we can't have that, can we?"

Reuben chuckled, dropping his gaze to the ground as a flush rose at his neck. He glanced up at Stenhouse and to the expectant McGuire gathering, nodded his head. "I'll be happy to oblige," and started toward the group, having tethered Blue on to a wagon wheel.

As he walked close to the group, Elly stepped away, smiling broadly at him, and motioning him close. "Reuben! I want you to meet my family," turning back to face her waiting parents. "This is my father, Jerome, my mother, Abigail, and my little sister, Phoebe." She turned back to Reuben. "Family, this is Reuben, the man that rescued us!" She slipped her hand under the crook of his arm and nudged him forward, smiling up at him.

"Pleased to meet you folks," he answered as he doffed his hat, nodding to the woman and girl. He extended his hand to shake with the father who nodded as he smiled broadly. "I don't know how we can ever thank you, Reuben. You've brought our daughter, who we thought was lost, back to us. We will be forever grateful." He vigorously shook Reuben's hand, clasping it in both his as he nodded to the younger man. He released his grip. "Please, please, come with us, the ladies will be fixing an early breakfast as the captain says we'll be leaving early, so join us."

While the women eagerly worked to prepare breakfast for their guest, the men sat together before the fire, getting acquainted. Reuben gave Jerome McGuire a short summary of his life, only touching upon his time in the war, while Jerome told of their life in Illinois before joining with the Mormons and starting the trek west. He nodded toward Elly. "She's had a few young men that have, shall we say, chased after her, but she never paid them no mind. Although she was not excited about our deciding to go to the promised land with the others, she knew her place was with her family, at least until she has a family of her own."

Reuben accepted a cup of steaming coffee from a smiling Elly, nodded his thanks and glanced to see her mother smiling and nodding. It was evident what the family was thinking but Reuben was beginning to feel a little uncomfortable. The little sister, bouncing around and acting a little giddy, even for a thirteen-year-old, came to Reuben's side and said, "Elly thinks you're handsome!"

Reuben chuckled. "That's because she hasn't seen me in the daylight. You see, when the sun comes out, I turn into a real ogre!" he frowned severely to emphasize his point, but the girl just laughed.

"Ain't no such thing!" she declared, "'Sides, it's time to eat!" and skipped to the crude bench beside the plank table as Elly and her mother sat the pans of food out. Phoebe pointed to the bench on the opposite side. "You and Elly sit there!" she instructed as she swung her legs around the end of the bench to scoot under the table.

Reuben glanced at Elly who had fixed her hair in long ringlet curls that hung to her shoulders and donned a different dress of gingham in a pale green pattern that seemed to suit her light skin. She smiled coyly as she came near to sit next to Reuben, and slipped onto the bench, swung her feet under the table as Reuben strad-dled the bench and sat beside her, setting his hat on the end of the bench beside him. Jerome stood at the end of the table. "Let us pray..." he began, and everyone joined hands and bowed their heads, Elly squeezing Reuben's hand as if to telegraph her feelings to him.

With a stack of Johnny cakes before him, Reuben tied into the meal with enthusiasm. He slathered butter and maple syrup over the top, took a big bite of fried pork belly, and began putting away the special treat. Elly smiled as she watched Reuben enjoy the feast and explained, "The butter we churned on the way, the Hastings have a milk cow that gives rich milk. And the maple syrup came from the trees on our farm in Illinois."

Reuben nodded, tried to finish the mouthful he was enjoying, and answered, "They sure are good!" He smiled and cut another big bite. "I haven't had Johnnycakes since 'fore I went to war," but the thought of the war and his family dampened his enthusiasm a little but did not slow his eating.

"I like a man with an appetite," declared Abigail, nodding at Reuben. "Our Elly fixed those Johnnycakes this morning. She's a fine cook."

"Ma!" whined Elly, frowning at her mother and shaking her head, but scooting a little closer to Reuben.

"Do you plan on settling down when you get out west, Reuben?" asked Abigail, glancing up and away, anxious for an answer.

"I'm not sure, ma'am. Don't rightly know where or when that'll be, at least not yet."

Elly looked at her mother. "Reuben is scouting for the wagon train behind us," and glanced at Reuben. "Aren't you?"

"Well, sort of, I've been ridin' ahead of them, kinda watchin' out for 'em. They've had some troubles and I've tried to help as I could."

"Surely you don't just ride around looking for

damsels in distress to go rescue, do you?" asked Abigail, frowning.

"No, ma'am, but sometimes it's kinda forced on me, like tonight. Couldn't hardly let the natives have the girls, now, could I?" he explained, extending his cup for another fill of coffee.

He sat back, looking around the table at the family. "Will you be farmin' when you get to Salt Lake, Jerome?"

"I don't rightly know, Reuben. Sometimes the church has other duties for us, but we'll see soon enough. We're still kind of new to the LDS, but we're learning and are committed, well, at least Abigail and I are; the girls, well, time will tell I suppose."

Reuben nodded his understanding, watched as the women cleared the table and caught Elly smiling at him quite often. He was feeling a little like a mouse in a trap, but he was enjoying being near Elly and he certainly liked the way she looked and the way she looked at him. There was something warm about being near her, something he had not experienced before, but he was also a little confused. He was not in a place in his life to be taking a wife, but...he liked being with Elly.

They walked together across the wagon formation, returning to where Reuben had tethered Blue. The stars were beginning to dim their lanterns, the moon was lowering in the west and the faint line of grey marked the eastern horizon. Reuben paused beside Blue, slipped the end of the rein from the wagon wheel, and turned to face Elly. She lifted her hands to Reuben's shoulders, looked up at him in the dim light. "You have a special place in my heart. I know we've only known each other for a short while, but I don't know, it's special. And not just because you came to our rescue, there's more, I feel we should be together."

Reuben slowly shook his head, looking down into the blue eyes that sparkled in the moonlight. "But how? We're in the middle of Indian country, and I have no idea where I'm goin' or what lies ahead." He breathed deep, cupping her elbows in his palms and pulling her close. "I don't understand it, but I feel somethin' special also."

She tiptoed and kissed him, prompting him to hold her close as he returned the embrace. She lay her head on his chest, clinging to the loose sleeves of his tunic, not wanting to let him go, but he pulled back to look down at her. "I've got some things to do with the other train. I will try to catch up to you after that's done, but..." he let the question and the possibilities hang between them.

Elly smiled up at him. "I will watch for you, and if you don't come, I'll be coming after you!" she declared firmly.

Reuben chuckled. "As long as you don't come with a gun!"

As he turned his back on the wagons, Reuben let his mind wander on the possibilities of his future. He had never thought much about taking a wife, settling down, although he assumed that was something that would happen eventually. But his thoughts had been more on the immediate future; what he would do today, tomorrow, maybe a week or two away, but further than that was left to circumstance, as is often the way of the young who assume they will live forever and have innumerable tomorrows.

The image of Elly kept coming to mind, how she looked and smiled, and the lilt of her voice and the way she had of looking at him with a twinkle in her eye and a smile tugging at the corner of her dimpled cheek. It was only when Blue came to a stop, his head lifted, that Reuben realized he was back at his camp. He looked at the pack mule, Jack, who had turned to look at him and Blue, and giving an expression of boredom, dropped his head for a mouthful of grass and chewed, his jaw appearing to dislocate with every bite. Reuben swung down, stripped the gear from Blue, let him roll and began rubbing him down with a handful of grass. He tethered the roan, rubbed his forehead, and said, "I wish you could tell me what to do, Blue. Pa always did say horses had more sense than people!" He chuckled at the memory, picturing his father leaning in the doorway of their home, and breathed deep as he reached for the binoculars and his Sharps.

He started up the back side of the knoll that stood beside the trail on the north bank of the Platte, the same one he used as a promontory when he saw the women taken by the Oglala. As he crested the knoll, he heard the crack of whips, the shouts of the ox handlers, and the creak of wheels as the wagons started on the trail. Sunrise was still about an hour away, but the dim light of pre-dawn was enough to keep them on the trail and give them a good start on the day's travel. Reuben watched as the wagons rolled, trying to spot the McGuire wagon, knowing Elly said she would be riding most of the day, probably riding the mustang taken from the Sioux. As he searched, he thought he had a glimpse of her beside the wagon, but the shadows from the sandhills and the close-by trees on the Platte Riverbank robbed him of one last look at the woman that had filled his thoughts.

For about three miles from the confluence of the Birdwood and the Platte, the Mormon trail was closely sandwiched between the sandhills and the thickets of the Platte. It was also a dangerous place for an ambush by the Oglala, but with their early start, the wagons should make it through that narrow defile and be well on their way come full daylight. Reuben watched them as long as he could, the white tops rocking with the gait of the oxen and the trail, making Reuben think they were waving a farewell. He shook his head, *Meet one woman for one night, and she's got your mind wanderin' ever which way!*

He sat back against the big sandstone slab and turned his gaze to the east, looking down the long valley of the North Platte, knowing the wagons of the folks from Kearny would be coming along sometime today and with that realization came the thoughts about the gun runners. As the sun began to paint the underbellies of the ragged clouds the pale pink of early morning, Reuben began mentally mapping the valley floor, searching for possible campsites for the train, believing they would stop nearby in anticipation of the trade with the Sioux. The most logical place would be on this, the north side of the river, but the Great Platte River Road or Oregon Trail hugged the south bank of the Platte while the Mormon trail stayed to the north.

He looked at the terrain and the trees, breaks in the thickets and crossing points over the river, trying to second guess where the traders would park the wagon. As he thought about the big Conestoga, he thought about the suggestion of McDonald to use the black powder. He was planning on placing the keg as McDonald suggested but was also concerned about any nearby wagons and people. Somehow, they would try to get the wagon to the Indians or...or what? *There's too many cases of rifles to try to move them any other way, it's got to be with the wagon.* He frowned at his own thoughts, wondering.

With no wagons in sight, Reuben rose from his observation post and started down the slope, but movement near the creek caught his attention. He stopped, looking to the shady side of the trees this side of the creek and saw three deer making their way to water for their morning drink. With another look back up the valley, anticipating the Sioux to come storming down any time seeking vengeance on the wagon train with the women, he did not want to expose himself, but fresh venison was mighty tempting.

He worked his way around the point of the knoll, staying close to the cover of scattered juniper and cedar, saw the last deer of the bunch stop and lift his head in his direction, revealing himself as a button buck. Reuben waited till the buck turned and started toward the trees, then snatched up his rifle for a quick aim and shot, dropping the animal with a neck shot and sending the others scampering away. He made quick work of dressing out the buck, scattered the entrails in the brush for the scavengers but out of sight of passersby, and hefted the hide bundle of meat to his shoulder to go back to camp.

He hung the meat in the high branches of a big juniper, keeping it in the shade even in the heat of the day, and would wait until after whatever was to happen with the wagons before he would try to smoke it or cure it in any way. He thought of the families with the train and thought he might try to visit with them before he decided what he would do about the rifles. But for now, it had been a long night, the sun was chasing the leftover clouds from the sky, and he needed some rest. He rolled out his blankets in the shade of the rocky ledge and the gnarly cedar that stood atop it, and trusting his animals to stand watch, covered his eyes with his hat and went to sleep.

It was early afternoon before he roused from his snooze, the sun was peeking through the branches of the cedar, trying to paint his face with bright sunlight and the warmth stirred him awake. He looked slowly around his camp, saw the roan and mule standing hipshot with their heads in the shade of the juniper, and nothing amiss, so he stretched, and rose from his blankets. He slipped the gold pocket watch from his pocket, snapped the cover open and saw it was crowding two o'clock. He glanced at the sun and started absent-mindedly winding the watch, thinking of his father and how he always carried this same watch whether working in the field or sitting in the pew at church.

Blue and Jack were on long tethers, able to reach the trickle of water that came from the spring and the grassy knob sheltered by the trees, and satisfied they were doing alright, Reuben picked up his Sharps, the telescope sights, and his binoculars and started up the knob for another look around. As he crested the knoll, he dropped to a crouch, made his way to the sandstone slab and the cedar, and took his place beside the big rock. With the rifle cradled in his lap, he put his elbows on his knees and lifted the binoculars for a search of the valley of the Platte.

Reuben knew from McDonalds Stage stop to the Birdwood Creek was more than a day's travel, but less than two, unless they had some trouble or made some excuse for stopping short of a full day's travel. But he also did not know how close they were to McDonald's before they stopped, or if they made it a point to spend any time at the trading post of McDonald. Based on their rate of travel thus far, it would be reasonable to expect them to make a stop near the confluence of the fresh-water creek.

He scanned from the confluence back to the east, downstream of the river, searching both the flats and the tree line for any sign of life. Directly east of his position, about ten miles back, he remembered the Platte took a wide bend to the southeast, to eventually come to the confluence of the north and south branches of the Platte. Almost directly below him, where the Birdwood met the Platte, the bigger river split and a smaller branch, not

155

much more than a shallow creek, twisted through the thicker woods to eventually re-join with the main branch about five or six miles downstream.

Where the Birdwood met the Platte, the big river made a dogleg bend to the south, straddling a flat island, and spreading out across a gravelly bottom crossing often used by wagons from either the Mormon trail or the Oregon trail. It was often used by the women for a laundry site, and the far edge held the freshwater feed from the Birdwood, prompting many to fill their water barrels. Reuben guessed it would be in that flat where the wagons would stop, offering the trees on the south bank of the dogleg as the usual choice for the Conestoga.

Movement caught Reuben's eye and he focused on a lone rider, making his way between the trail and the tree line, probably the scout for the wagons. He rode slumped in the saddle, obviously tired from a long day's ride, probably a bit bored with the monotonous land-scape and the warm sun on his shoulders and edging its way to peek under the brim of his hat. Reuben smiled, knowing what the rider was feeling, but also knowing how easy it is to be distracted by weariness just when it was even more necessary to be wary. Another flash of color caught Reuben's eye and he swung the field glasses across the river to see another rider, a native, riding at a canter directly toward him. *That's gotta be a warrior on his way to give the word about the wagons coming!*

He scooted around to take a look at the valley of the Birdwood, searching for the Oglala. But he could not see any other warriors, no smoke from a camp, nothing. He watched as the rider rounded the point of the knob at the mouth of the valley, followed him as he rode on the far side of the creek, often masked by the trees, and lost him in the thicker trees and brush. He kept his glasses on the area, but nothing moved. *The others must be in the trees, that's about where we found 'em with the women.*

He turned back to see the scout for the wagons, watching as he reined up and stepped down, leading his mount to the shallows of the river. After a moment, he mounted and came a little further, staying by the tree line and soon made it to the clearing near the gravel bottomed crossing. He stopped, leaned on his pommel and Reuben watched, noticing the rider was a young man, not the captain or any of the others he saw when he had his little confrontation with the leaders of the wagons. The young man stepped down, stretched, and let his horse crop a little grass, then mounted up again and started back to the wagons.

Reuben lifted his glasses to see in the distance what resembled a reticulated white snake, knowing it was the wagon train, coming along just as expected. He glanced to the sun, guessed the distance to be close to three, maybe four miles, and knew the wagons would be here just at the right time to make camp and allow the gun runners to make their meeting with the Oglala.

From Reuben's perspective atop the bald knob, it was evident the flats south of the river were part of the old riverbed. But the land was fertile, lush with new grass and thickets of berry bushes, saplings of cottonwoods, sycamore, and silver maple. The few mature trees provided cover for the new growth and the grassy flats were inviting to both traveler and game animals. He watched as the white topped wagons waddled their way close and formed up in a circle in the crook of the dogleg bend in the Platte, exactly where Reuben had thought they would. As they maneuvered into position, the big Conestoga bulled his way next to the tree line on the north edge of the clearing and the south bank of the river. The driver worked his way around, so the wagon sided the trees close-in, with the tailgate almost under the tallest cottonwood. Reuben grinned as the man finished his maneuvering, dropped the lines, and crawled down from his lofty perch on the spring seat. The big Conestoga dwarfed the usual prairie schooner type of wagon, often fashioned, and rigged from farm wagons, and the six-up team of mules had proved their worth in the haul thus far.

The many men were busy stripping harness from the animals, taking them to water, rubbing them down and more, while the women started their now familiar routine of building the cookfire, often sending youngsters into the trees for firewood. Some of the wagons showed sagging bellies with hammocks of buffalo chips swinging underneath, cookfire fuel for camps where firewood was scarce, as was often the case with so many wagons traveling this trail over the past decade and more. Most of the woods had been picked clean and the only wood was from fresh winter kill trees and brush, but find it they did, and fires were soon flaring.

As long as there was light, Reuben determined to keep a watch on the wagons, especially the big Conestoga with the cargo of rifles. But he also kept a look-out for the Oglala, who by now knew the wagons had stopped for the night and could be readying to make their move. The sun was slipping below the western horizon, sending long lances of silver and gold heavenward. The blue-sky glowed orange and gold as the golden orb disappeared, and the light faded. Reuben took a last look up the valley, rose to a crouch and worked his way down the back side of the knoll, returning to his animals. As he moved, he thought, and a glance to the hide full of fresh meat gave him an idea.

He saddled Blue, packed the mule, and rode from the camp, dusk slowly dimming the remaining light. He nudged Blue into the water, pulling the lead on the mule taut, and slowly moved across the muddy river. The water was not quite belly deep here, and the bottom was sound, allowing them to cross with nothing more than the ripple of water moving against the legs of the animals. They climbed the bank where the trees were dense, slowly moved through the brush and grass to draw closer to the wagons. Reuben reined up, stepped down and loosely tethered the animals. He took the hide bundle of meat, removed some and replaced it with the keg of powder, replaced the meat atop and lifted the heavy burden to his shoulder.

Taking advantage of every bit of cover, he moved stealthily nearer, but not wanting to appear as if he were sneaking up on the wagons but trying to look as one of the men returning with meat. As he moved through the trees near the big wagon, he stumbled, quickly removed the keg of powder, hiding it in the brush, then stood and continued. His hat pulled low on his brow, rifle in his free hand, he hummed a tune as he walked from the trees toward the wagons. A quick glance showed the wagon of the colored family, the Hightowers, and he moved closer. When he neared the wagon, he called out, "Hiram, got some meat here for you."

Hiram Hightower turned to the voice, recognized Reuben and his eyes grew wide, "Why, you're the," but was hushed by Reuben's finger at his mouth.

"Thought you might use this," interrupted Reuben, dropping the bundle and opening it to reveal the fresh meat.

Hiram looked at the bundle, back at Reuben, spoke softly, "You brought that other meat too, did'nchu?"

"Ummhmm, got some more for my own self, but didn't think too many folks wanted to see me." Reuben looked to an upturned log beside the wagon. "Alright if I sit down?"

"Yessuh, yessuh," answered Hiram, motioning to the

makeshift stool. He turned to his wife. "Hannah, lookee here. Got some fresh meat!"

His wife looked up from her fixings, saw Reuben and looked wide-eyed at her man, saw him motioning to the bundle at his feet and rose to see. When she came near, she smiled at Reuben, nodding her head, looked at the bundle and said, "Thank you, Jesus!" as she lifted her eyes heavenward. "This be a mighty fine gift, suh, yessuh," smiling at Reuben.

"Enjoy it, ma'am. I thought you might use it, too much for me." He looked at Hiram, nodded to another log, "Mind if we talk?"

Hiram walked to the log, took a seat, and looked at Reuben, who spoke in low tones as not to scare Hiram's wife. "Last night, across the river there, another wagon train, larger than this one, Mormons they were, had some Indians steal some of their women that had gone into the trees lookin' for berries and such."

Hiram's eyes grew wide as he looked nervously to his wife and twin girls that were helping their mother. He looked back at Reuben. "Will they attack us?"

"I don't think so, but it would be best if you kept your weapons close at hand. The girls were rescued, and the train left before first light, but the Oglala have a village about ten miles up that valley yonder," nodding to the north across the river. "They might be wantin' some vengeance after some of their men were killed, but I think they're more interested in what's in that wagon yonder," nodding to the Conestoga. "Was anything done about what I said the other day?"

"Uh, no suh. The captain and the major, they said they talked to the man with the wagon, said he was settin' up a tradin' store and had farm stuff and some rifles for the settlers. He said most o' them boxes had farm stuff and Bibles and such."

"Ummhmmm, Beecher's Bibles, maybe," mumbled Reuben, shaking his head.

A voice called out from the front of the wagon, "Hiram? You around?" A smiling face peeked around the front. "There you are! Just checkin' on you, everythin' all right," asked the man as he came around the wagon. He glanced at Reuben, nodded, then frowned. "You're the man that spoke up for George Betts!" and walked closer, hand outstretched.

Reuben stood, accepting the offered hand, as the man continued, "Thank you for that. If you hadn't been there, no tellin' what might have happened."

Hiram stood, looked to Reuben. "Reuben, this is Pastor Wycliffe." He turned to the pastor, "Reuben is the one that brought the meat for us last time, and lookee here," pointing to the bundle, "there's more!"

"Well, praise the Lord! You *are* a blessin'!" he sat down on a stub of a bench, looking at Reuben, "Are you joinin' up with us now?"

"No, I don't think so. I just wanted to drop off some meat and talk to Hiram about a few things."

The pastor frowned, looking from Hiram to Reuben, until Hiram spoke softly, "Reuben said some Indians hit another wagon train just last night, right over yonder," pointing across the river.

"No, surely not," replied the pastor looking at Reuben.

"Yes, they did. They stole five of their young women, but they were rescued. It was the Mormon train, travelin' the road over there, and they left out before first light this mornin'."

"Do you think they'll hit our wagons? If so, we must

warn the people!"

"There's no tellin', but before you put the fear in the people and get the women folks all upset, it might be best to just warn a few, quietly, and make sure they have their weapons handy. I don't think the Oglala will strike, but, like I said, there's just no way of knowin' for sure."

"Reuben thinks they are wanting to trade for the rifles that the big wagon's carrying," offered Hiram.

The pastor looked from Hiram to Reuben. "But they said there were very few rifles, that most of that was farm equipment and Bibles for the missions and church-es." He looked to Reuben. "You still think they're wantin' to stir up the natives with rifles?"

"You ever hear of Beecher's Bibles, preacher?"

His eyes flared wide, quickly looking from Reuben to Hiram. "Yes! That was what the abolitionist minister, Henry Beecher, called the boxes with rifles they shipped to the anti-slavery fighters."

"Ummhmm, but there aren't any of those folks in the west, at least not fightin' about it."

"But what can we do about it? Most of the people on this train are fleein' the war."

"Nothin'. We don't know for sure what's goin' to happen until it does, but, if those rifles get into the hands of the Oglala, there won't be a wagon train safe for years to come." Reuben shook his head, looking around. "Just go to some of the men you can trust not to get all riled up, caution them to be on their guard and keep their weapons handy. I'll be watchin' for the natives and what might happen, just stay clear of the big wagon yonder."

The pastor looked at Reuben, back to Hiram and the men nodded their head as Reuben rose to leave. He shook hands with the men, and quickly stepped around the wagon and faded into the darkness of the trees. He moved through the thickets as silently as the night breeze, shadows mingling with shadows as dusk tucked itself away below the horizon. The big moon, now full, stood a hand's breadth above the eastern flats, the stars were lighting their lanterns, and the silence of the night lay upon the treetops like a comforting blanket.

Reuben moved nearer the big wagon, heard men talking and stepped closer. Near to the front of the wagon but apart from the others, a small fire licked at the chunks of wood, lighting the faces of the men gathered close. Reuben recognized the major, captain, and the driver of the Conestoga, but he could not get close enough to understand what was said. He looked at the wagon, saw the hammock hanging beneath, mostly empty, and noted the back end of the wagon was in the dark.

He stepped back into the dark, went to retrieve the keg of powder and quietly moved back near the wagon. He looked at the hammock, seen only by the light of the fire beyond that made a shadow of it, and the brush between him and the wagon. He mentally picked his way close, looked beneath the wagon, and judged if the keg would fit, and if it would be visible enough for a long shot. He breathed deep, stilling his nerves, and started to step forward but was stayed by a man walking around the back of the wagon. It was the driver and Reuben silently shrunk back into the dark shadows. He stood completely still, daring only to breathe, as he watched the man loosen the chains, heard them rattle and watched as he lowered the tailgate, squeaking and creaking as the hinges complained. The driver climbed into the wagon, shuffled some things about, and came out, sat on the tailgate, and dropped to the ground. He lifted the gate, fastened it, and walked back to the fire.

Reuben heard the man exclaim, "Everything's set. The powder and shot is on top, the crates of ammo underneath, and the boxes of Springfield's on the bottom. We can..." and his voice faded as he stepped closer to the fire and away from the wagon.

There was no mistaking the intent of the men now. If Reuben had any misgivings or doubts, they faded into the darkness as he stood thinking about what he heard. *Powder and shot on top, ammunition...* But no matter what was there, or what he might add to the mix, it meant nothing if it could not be set off before it got into the hands of the Oglala. Reuben sat the keg down, dropped to one knee to think through what he was planning. He eyed the wagon, saw the shadows of the men near the fire, considered whether it would be best to try to place the keg now, or wait until later, when most were asleep. But if he waited, the Oglala might...might what? Attack? Make the trade?

He shook his head, dropped to all fours to look under the wagon at the men by the fire, noted their positions and knew they were all facing the fire, probably staring at the flames, making their night vision useless, and none were facing the wagon. He looked at the rest of the camp, the other wagons were further away since the driver of the Conestoga let it be known he preferred to be off by himself. Reuben grinned at the thought of the man thinking his desire for solitude just might be his undoing.

With a deep breath, Reuben hoisted the keg to his shoulder, and staying low, using his knees and one hand, he moved silently toward the wagon, letting the shadows cast by the rising moon keep him in darkness. When he was beside the rear wheel, he lowered the keg, slid between the wheels, and rolled the keg close. With another glance to the men at the fire, he lay on his back and lifted the keg into the hammock, carefully moving it into the low sag, and covering it with handfuls of grass to mask the shape if a careless glance looked that way. With another look at the fire, he started to roll from under the wagon, but feet near the wagon stopped him and he froze in place.

The legs showed it to be the woman, standing by the tool chest mounted on the side of the wagon. Apparently having commandeered the tool chest for her clothes, she was mumbling to herself, and Reuben saw her drop a couple items of clothing, fuss some more, then as he watched, she stripped off her dress, dropped the petti-coat and a few other items Reuben did not know the name of, and stood by the wagon in her underdrawers as she fussed some more, then began donning other cloth-ing. Reuben had moved back from the wheels, pulled some grasses high and over him, and watched as she bent over to retrieve the cast-off garments. She snatched them up, not looking his way, stuffed them in the chest, dropped the lid, and stomped off. Reuben grinned, shaking his head, and quickly rolled from under the wagon and disappeared into the shadows of the trees.

As he returned to his horse and mule, he mentally pictured the location of the wagon, the trees nearby and where he would have to be to get a clear shot at the keg underneath. The only possible angle would have to come from across the clearing, behind the wagons and hopefully in the trees. But to get there, he would not be in position to see the Oglala. He swung aboard Blue, reined him back to the river and nudged him into the water, leading the mule on a loose lead. The moon bounced gold nuggets off the ripples and cast long shadows on the far bank, leaving the rest of the terrain in silvery blue light.

They moved quietly from the water, went into the trees to move downstream on the north bank before crossing back to the south bank and into the trees. But something stopped him, that crawling sensation at his back that had saved him many times before, and Blue had paused, looking about. He reined up, leaned low on Blue's neck, and whispered, "Easy boy, what's out there?"

The roan had bent his neck back to the left, his ears pricked forward, his head high and his nostrils flaring. They were well hidden in the trees, both mule and horse standing stock still and watching toward the mouth of the valley of the Birdwood. The moonlight let shadows dance as several riders came from the edge of the creek, moving slowly and quietly, and the shadows of others moved on the far bank, going to the trees beside the big river. The Oglala moved quietly, until the leader lifted his hand to stop the band before they reached the tree line on the shore. They sat a moment, listening, until the leader cupped his hands to his mouth and gave a perfect mimic of the call of the night hawk. They listened a few moments, he gave another call, and sat waiting. Within a moment, the hoot of a great horned owl pierced the night, and the Oglala nodded, moved his mount into the water, followed by four of his warriors, but a motion from the leader kept the others where they sat.

Reuben also remained motionless. Even though he and his animals could move quietly through the woods, the movement in the shadows would be a giveaway. And with so many listening, no sound would go undetected. But Reuben knew the few that had crossed the river could not carry more than a few of the rifles, the wagon would have to either leave the rifles in the trees, and move away, or...and Reuben realized that was what would happen, they would leave the rifles and take the wagon and move away, with the keg of powder underneath. Somehow, he had to get in a position to set off the powder before they moved the rifles. Surely they would not try to unload with the other wagons and men nearby, someone might suspect something.

Reuben lay low on Blue's neck, rolled to the far side, and stepped down. He looked through the trees to the waiting Oglala, back at the roan and the mule, and chose to try to move them further into the trees away from the warriors. It would be risky, but if he left them, and one moved even slightly, they could be seen. Standing at the head of Blue, he stroked the roan's face and jaw, whispering to him as he did and slowly moved back a half-step. With a glance toward the Oglala, he knew they were in the dark shadows, the brush, and trees thick, but he moved slowly. One step, pause, another, pause, and was starting another when the splashing of water told of the return of the other warriors.

Reuben stepped around Blue, looked through the trees to see the five men come from the river, speak to the others and with a hand motion held high to signal those on the far bank, the entire band turned and started back into the valley of the Birdwood. With a heavy sigh, Reuben mounted up and nudged Blue into the trees to make the wide swing around the camp of the wagons, and cross back over the river to find a spot to make his shot.

He took up his position in a cluster of cottonwood saplings with service berry bushes around the base of the young trees. In broad daylight, it would not be the best position, and the saplings, none much bigger around than the calf of his leg, would not provide much protection from a rifle assault, but it put him in a good position to make the necessary shot. With his animals tethered back in the thicker trees, he settled into his spot, sat back on his haunches, and watched the wagons. The full moon gave him a good view of the big wagon, his angle gave him a good line of sight. He finished attaching his telescopic sight, the mounting setting the scope to the side of the barrel leaving the open sights visible and usable if necessary.

Once the rifle and scope were secure, he lay the weapon across his lap, and lifted his eyes to the wagons. A glance to his right showed the dim grey at the horizon making silhouettes of the hills in the east. It would be daylight soon and the wagons, on a usual day, would be on the move with first light. He looked back to the wagons, saw movement among the group, a few women were stirring up the coals from the previous night, men began sorting out the harnesses, making a check of the wheels, axles, and hardware of the wagons. A few were making their trek to the trees for their morning constitutional, but nothing moved by the Conestoga.

Reuben frowned, lifted his field glasses for a closer look, but the light was too dim, the shadows too dark, to show anything more than what he could see without the glasses. A golden eagle circled overhead, watching the activity, searching for some varmint for his breakfast, let out his cry that pierced the dim light and startled

Reuben. He looked up to see the big bird tuck his wings and make his dive toward the flats away from the trees. Reuben watched the magnificent bird swoop down, snatch a young rabbit in his talons, and lift back to the sky, his prey kicking and squealing.

Reuben grinned, shook his head at the way of things, and looked to the wagons. There was movement at the Conestoga, the driver was walking around the wagon, stopped, and stood staring at the front wheel, kicked at it and made a ruckus that was noticed by others who came near. He saw the gestures, and recognized the man was talking to the pastor, hands on hips when they were not waving in the air or pointing at the wheel. The pastor shook his head, lifted his arms in resignation, and walked away.

Reuben grinned, knowing the driver was setting the stage for his remaining behind to work on the wheel, probably offering to catch up with the rest of the wagons later. Since there had been no activity at the wagon throughout the night, Reuben knew the cases of rifles were still on board and knew the plan must be for the wagon to stay behind, offload the rifles and ammunition, then catch up with the rest of the train, probably with empty cases aboard.

Reuben's stomach was growling with hunger as he watched several of the families taking their breakfast while others were already hitching the horses or mules to the wagons, readying for their departure. A quick glance to his right showed the brilliant colors of the morning sky, shades of red splashed across the cloudless sky giving the impression that the eastern horizon was afire. Reuben remembered the old adage, *Red sky at morning, sailors take warning. Red sky at night, sailor's delight.* Perhaps it was the hand of God that painted the sky this morning.

The crack of whips, the shouts of drivers, announced the stretching out of the train, and as expected the Conestoga sat alone, mules tethered at the trees close to the water and fresh grass and well away from the wagon. Reuben watched as the train stretched out, saw the captain and major sitting astride their mounts, watching the wagons pass. As the last wagon rounded the point of trees at the edge of the clearing, the men still sat, watching the wagons move along the trail that sided the south bank of the Platte. He remembered the trail was separated from the river by the tree cover and would angle almost directly west until the hills to both the south and north pushed the river into a narrow cut, forcing the trail to almost ride the riverbank. But that was about two to three miles further upstream to the west.

The two men sat their horses, watching the wagons move out, talking to one another until the last wagon was about a half mile distant. The major reined his mount around and started back to the Conestoga. It was then that Reuben noticed the driver of the Conestoga was lowering the tailgate, and Reuben lifted the Sharps.

As he remembered, the keg hung below the belly of the wagon about a foot, and with a diameter of about twelve to fifteen inches, his target, although over three hundred yards distant, was larger than the ten-inch target he had to hit from two hundred yards just to qualify for the Sharpshooters. He set the triggers, narrowed his sight target using the telescopic sight, took a slow breath, let out a little, and slowly squeezed off the shot.

The big Sharps bucked, roared, spat smoke and fire,

and sent the .52 caliber slug on its way. In an instant, the keg exploded, erupting under the wagon, and setting off the powder and ammunition within the wagon. Reuben watched as the huge cloud billowed grey and black, the wagon shattered into shards, the canvas caught fire as it wafted up like a mushroom, and the impact was felt under the ground beneath him. Mules screamed and brayed, breaking their tethers and running from the trees, necks stretched out, teeth bared, eyes flaring and tails waving. The debris rained down, the largest piece Reuben saw was part of the spring seat floating down, twisting in the air and driving into the dirt to stand like a headstone at a grave.

He had not watched the approach of the captain and the major, but saw their horses staggering, limping, heads hanging and the men nowhere to be seen. There was no sign of the driver of the wagon, nor the woman that rode with him pretending to be his wife. Reuben sat silent, shaking his head at the destruction. He had not expected the blast to be so strong nor so destructive. He only wanted to destroy the rifles, but the crater where the wagon had been told of how the force of one keg of powder had been multiplied by the powder and ammunition aboard the wagon.

He sat watching the dust and powder cloud slowly dissipate and as he looked, the Oglala came from the trees, looking around, gesturing, and talking, obviously angry, but pacified somewhat when they spotted the bodies of the captain and major. There was nothing to do, nothing to take, nothing of value or use left, and the Indians rode into the trees and could be heard crossing the river.

R euben waited a bit for any sign of the natives' return and rose from his point to go to the horses. Although he was not anxious to do it, he knew the right thing would be to check for the remains and bury what was left. He swung aboard Blue, reined him around and with the mule on a loose lead pointed Blue to the scene of the blast. He carefully negotiated among the debris, spotted what he thought was a body and stepped down, ground tied the roan and walked closer. Within about fifteen feet of one another lay the bodies of the captain and the major, both somewhat mutilated and recognizable only by the shreds of clothing still familiar. He would look for the horses later. A few steps closer to the crater and he knew there would be nothing remaining of the driver and the woman. Reuben shook his head, returned to the mule, and retrieved his pack shovel to go to the edge of the trees and start digging a grave.

He was filling in the grave where both bodies lay when a rider came around the point headed his direction. He saw it was not an Indian and assumed it would be someone from the wagons returning because of the blast. Asa Hampton, the older of the Hampton brothers, rode close, saw Reuben filling in the grave and stopped, leaned over his pommel, and asked, "What happened?"

Reuben paused, looked at the young man. "You from the wagons?"

"Yessir, I'm Asa Hampton. The captain had me'n a couple others doin' the outriders job, since the others were kilt. I came back lookin' for the captain."

Reuben nodded to the grave. "There he be, the major too."

"Noo," drawled the young man, astonished at the thought. He looked at the crater. "Was that the big wagon?"

"Ummhmmm. The one that didn't have any rifles and ammunition or powder and such. Musta been all them Bibles. I've heard the Word of God is quick and powerful," proclaimed Reuben, resuming his burial detail.

"Well, I'll be a prickly backed porcupine. If that don't beat all!"

"You'll be a scalped porcupine if you don't hurry on back to the wagons and let 'em know the Oglala are a mite stirred up since they didn't get their rifles."

"They wouldn't! We didn't have nothin' to do with that!"

"I don't think they will see it that way. You go on now, I'll be along a bit later. Make sure the wagons keep movin' and no stoppin' for noonin'. They need to get as far as they can 'fore dark. Go on now, you're in charge!"

The young man sat up, puffed his chest out. "I'm in charge?"

"That's right, at least until the rest of the folks decide different. Hurry on, now!" directed Reuben, waving the young man on his way. Asa slapped legs to his mount, reined around and took off, eager at his new responsibility. Anxious to prove himself.

Reuben finished the deed, covered the graves with a scattering of rocks and branches, made a last check of the area and the debris, and turning away, rode from the site, a heaviness weighing upon his shoulders and his mind. He never thought he could do what he did, three men and one woman dead, but he had to do it. If the rifles had gotten into the hands of the restive Oglala, warriors intent on vengeance and more, there was no way to count how many lives would have been lost. He tried to remember the encouragement of Parson Page, how there are times when God has to raise up his own warriors to stay the forces of evil, and what he was intent on doing was just that, to stop the evil he had encountered. He sighed heavily, shoulders heaving, as he shook his head and tried to focus on the future.

The wagons still had a long way to go just to get to Fort Laramie, probably about two weeks or more travel, and to get there meant going through the land of the Lakota Sioux, the Arapaho to the south and the Cheyenne who were nearer the fort. Jim Bridger had schooled Reuben on what to expect between Kearny and Fort Laramie and he took it to heart, concerned for both the wagon train of the Mormons and those from Fort Kearny.

He was not in a hurry to catch up to the wagons, although he knew they would want to know more about the explosion and the threat of the Sioux. He let Blue have his head and was comfortable with the horse's chosen gait, for neither Blue nor Reuben were anxious to be with other people. When the river pushed close to the rolling hills to the south, Reuben nudged Blue to a shallow draw that held a trickle of water and ample fresh spring growth grass. He stepped down, picketed the animals, and started up the slope of the nearest hill. The land had become more barren, where before there were juniper and cedar, now there was bunch grass, sage, and cacti.

Once atop the crest, he guessed he was no more than sixty or seventy feet higher than the valley floor, but it was enough to give him an advantageous view of the surroundings. He was mostly concerned about any pursuing Oglala and searched the back trail as well as the trail on the far side of the river, but there was no sign of the Sioux. He turned to look upstream after the wagons, but they were too far away to be seen. He found he was a little relieved at not seeing them, whether it was because he knew he would have to face them regarding the explosion, or if he was just relieved to not see a circle of burning wagons set upon by warring Sioux. He thought about the Mormon train and Elly, wondering if they were alright and avoiding the warlike natives. He smiled at the memory of the girl, picturing her clearly before him in her pale green gingham dress and long curls. He shook his head. *She sure is pretty!*

As he walked down the slope to Blue and Jack, he realized how tired he was, but he could not use them for an excuse to rest up. While he had been keeping watch all night, they had been sleeping and now were raring to go and put some miles behind them. He chuckled to himself, mounted up and took to the trail.

By midday, the clouds had gathered and offered a little respite from the hot sun, a bit of a breeze added to the relief and Reuben stayed to the trail. He reckoned he had covered about twelve or fifteen miles when he started to take a break, get a bite to eat and rest the animals a spell, but in the distance, he spotted the white snake of the wagon train, on the move. He shook his head and determined to take to the shade of the trees near the river and get some food and coffee. There was plenty of time to catch the wagons.

With a snippet of a fire, he had his little coffee pot dancing, and the thin sliced strips of venison backstrap were sizzling over the flames, dangling from the willow withes. His stomach was telling him to hurry with the food and he snatched a small tidbit, tossed it from hand to hand, held it gingerly with fingertips and blew on it, then popped it in his mouth to shush the growling stomach. He smacked his lips and reached for another and within just a few minutes, the fire had dwindled to coals, the pot stopped its dance, and the willows were bare. He sat back, rubbed his stomach, and lifted his cup to his lips, blew on the hot brew, and sipped it down.

But he had no sooner started to sit back and savor the moment, than Blue became a little skittish, turning to look at him and looking down the tree line, ears pricked and nostrils flaring. Reuben came to his feet, shaded his eyes to look, but saw nothing alarming. He picked the field glasses from the saddle bags, stepped away from the trees to look in the direction that had alarmed Blue, but whatever had alarmed him was too far to be seen. He quickly doused the fire, stuffed the pot in the pack, and swung aboard the now prancing Blue. He started to slap his legs to let the roan run, but before he could lift them, the big blue roan was stretching out, the mule keeping pace just a half-length back.

The white tops of the wagons just came in sight, and he recognized they had circled up. He glanced to the sun, saw it was still a couple hours before day's end, and heard the first shots, followed by screaming war cries. Blue heard the same sounds and seemed to double his efforts, lunging into a ground eating gallop, mane flying as Reuben lay along the roan's neck. He made a quick scan of the area, saw the wagons were pinned near the edge of the hills at a bottleneck between the river and the rolling hills. Reuben nodded to himself, leaned toward the round tops to steer Blue that way, and nudged him to take to a low sloping hillock. Without missing a step, the long-legged roan lunged up the slope, humping his back, stretching with all he had, until they crested the mound and Reuben swung down, Sharps rifle in hand.

With the Roan, sides heaving and lather dripping, ground tied on the low side of the mound, Reuben went to one knee and lifted the big Sharps. He took a sight on the first Indian he saw, followed him an instant and dropped the hammer. The big gun bucked and spat lead, knocking the warrior from his mount, tumbling end over end to be trampled by another warrior's riderless horse. Before the first target stopped tumbling, Reuben had reloaded and was taking aim at another target. A warrior was charging straight for a break between wagons and Reuben's slug pierced his back, smashing out the man's chest and taking his bone pipe breast plate with it, dropping the man underneath the wagon tongue he had intended to jump his horse over. The body never moved, and Reuben quickly reloaded.

The rifle fire from the wagons was like rolling thunder, the screams and war cries from the Oglala were barely heard, but the leaders of the Sioux sent wave after wave of attackers charging toward the wagons, only to have them turned back by the wall of fire and lead. The terrain about the wagons was littered with bodies of both men and horses, but there was no lull in the battle. Reuben looked beyond the wagons where the attacks were emanating and spotted a group of what he supposed were chiefs that were directing the battle. He calculated the distance to be about seven or eight hundred yards, far enough that the chiefs thought themselves safe, but Reuben just nodded, his lip lifting in a snarl as he lowered the muzzle of the Sharps, steadied his hold with his elbow on his knee, and slowly brought the focus of the telescopic sight to bear on the center figure of the leaders of the Sioux.

He paused, moving the sight to the other chiefs, returned to his first choice and steadied his aim. He drew in a slow breath, let out a bit, and slowly squeezed the thin trigger. The rifle bucked, belched, and bellowed as it sent the bullet on its way. Reuben brought the scope sight to bear on the target just as the bullet blossomed red on the chest of the chief, whose eyes flared, mouth dropped open and he slowly fell backwards over the rump of his horse. The other leaders, startled though they were, looked for the shooter, searching the nearby trees and the land before them. While they jabbered among themselves, looking at their fallen comrade, another leader grunted, bent sideways and fell to the ground.

Reuben quickly reloaded for his third try at the distant leaders, but when he lifted the rifle again, they were gone, and the warriors had turned from their attack and were retreating to the tree line. Reuben picked one of the stragglers, dropped the hammer and sent another of the attackers to the great beyond. He lowered the rifle, realized he was breathing heavy and sat back on his rump, watching the people of the wagons scurry about, tending their wounded and more. He saw a few of the warriors trying to drag themselves away from the flats and out of sight of the wagons, and chose to let them go, their fight was gone out of them.

He walked back to Blue, slipped the Sharps in the scabbard, and swung aboard. He reined the roan around and started back down the slope, bound for the wagons. As he neared, he called out, "Hello the wagons!"

An answering cry came, "Come on in, Reuben," and he recognized the voice as that of Hiram Hightower. The man lifted the tongue of his wagon to admit Reuben and his animals, dropped it behind him and restacked the boxes alongside. Hiram came to his side as he stepped down and started to look around. "Lost a couple o' folks," nodding to the small group gathered by one wagon. One of the men looked up, saw Reuben, and came over.

Pastor Wycliffe extended his hand. "Welcome Reuben. Thanks for what you did up there," nodding toward the hillside. "I saw you ride in and go up there, heard the big boom of your Sharps and knew you were doin' your part."

"Wish I coulda done more, Pastor," answered Reuben, quietly, noticing the grieving among the group. "Who'd you lose?"

"A couple, Herbert and Amy Fredericks. She was loadin' the rifles for her husband, he was at the front, there," nodding to where the group was gathered, the point of attack for the Oglala. "And Gertie Brown and her son, Ebenezer. He was twelve, I believe. Her husband, Arthur, is takin' it mighty hard. He's left with his daughter, Tabitha, I think she's ten."

"Well, Pastor, you're needed there. Don't let me keep you."

The pastor nodded, turned away and went to the

second of the two groups where Arthur Brown was grieving over his wife's body held in his lap. Reuben knew this was going to be hard on all of them, but it had to be done. They had to get away from this place before the band chose other leaders and returned for even more vengeance and retaliation. He looked for the young man he met back at the wagon, spotted Asa Hampton, caught his eye and motioned him over. The young man nodded and started his direction. Reuben breathed heavy, knowing he was going to be hated for this, but it had to be done.

"We'll go together, but we've got to get the wagons movin', put some distance between us and the Oglala," directed Reuben, speaking to Asa Hampton, one of the young men chosen as outriders.

"You really think they'll come back? Hit us again?" asked the youth.

"Nobody would know for sure, but we can't take that chance. There's more warriors back at their village and they're mad enough to want to wipe out this entire wagon train. There's plenty of their dead out there now, and they'll be back for them, and we need to be long gone when they do."

"Alright, if you think it's best," allowed the young man.

At the first wagon, they met Joshua Becker, His wife Isabella was tending a minor wound on the man's arm as they looked up to see the two approach. "Howdy, Asa, your folks alright?" asked Joshua.

"Yes, Mr. Becker. They did fine, but we're here to tell you the wagons'll be movin' out right soon, and you best get 'er hitched up and ready."

"Movin' out? Why it's pert' near dark! Why we movin' anyway?" asked the man, looking from Asa to Reuben. "Say, ain'tchu the one what kilt them others?"

"That's right. But the wagons need to get movin' before the Oglala come back. They've got about a hundred more warriors back at their village and if they decide to come back, I don't think this few will prevail," suggested Reuben.

Their conversation had drawn the attention of the men from the nearby wagons who came close to listen and one man chimed in, "Why would they come back? We whupped 'em the first time. You'd think they'd know better." It was George Betts, the man who threw the meat clever and stopped Bull Pawlak from taking his wife.

"You didn't whip them. They left because two of their leaders were killed, back by the trees yonder, and they needed to choose new leaders, before resumin' the fight."

The men frowned, looked where Reuben motioned, and Joshua Becker said, "We couldn'ta done that, why that's oe'r two hundred yards away. We was shootin' at them comin' at us, not oe'r yonder!"

"This is no time to argue the details, get your wagons hitched and ready to move out. We'll pull out in a half hour, maybe sooner," stated Reuben, motioning to Asa to come with him to the other wagons.

As they walked off, the men at the Becker wagon looked at one another, "I don't rightly know 'bout that fella. Who does he think he is tellin' us what to be doin'?" His sons, Malachi, who also served as an outrider, and the younger son, Abraham, looked askance at their father. "Son," began Joshua, and speaking to Malachi, "You run on over there an' see if there's any dead injuns there." Malachi nodded, and took off at a run, carrying his rifle at his side.

Within a brief moment, Malachi came at a run back to the wagons and before he stopped, "Pa, Pa, there's two dead Indians there, just like he said, and they got feathers and such like a chief or sumpin'."

Joshua shook his head, looked at George Betts and the two other men that had joined them, "Well, fellas, I reckon we oughta be hitchin' up the teams. Don't know how far they'll be able to take us, but we best be gettin' ready." The others answered only by their quick stepping back to their wagons and packing the gear. The teams were all in the middle of the circle and as they began milling about, the men were picking their teams and leading them back to the wagons.

Reuben and Asa continued to the other wagons, spreading the word about leaving and several saw the others readying and quickly agreed and started their own chores. It wasn't until they came to the wagon of Arthur Brown, who lost his wife and son, that they were questioned again. "We can't be leaving! I've got to bury my wife and boy!" proclaimed Arthur Brown, shaking his head, tears still cutting furrows down the dusty face.

"Mr. Brown, we'll take your loved ones with us, bury them when it's safe. But we must be movin', as Reuben says," encouraged Pastor Wycliffe, his hand on Brown's shoulder.

The grieving man jerked back from the pastor, glared at Reuben. "Why'd they attack us, anyway?" he growled. "Was it cuz o' what you said back there?"

"This is not the time to try to figure that out. If the wagons don't get movin', the Oglala will probably be back to finish the job they started! Do you want to lose the rest of your family?" asked Reuben, trying not to be harsh or demanding, but needing to get the man moving.

Brown looked from Reuben to his daughter, held close by the pastor's wife, Martha and daughter, Lydia. "No, no. I'll get 'em hitched," he answered meekly, but his temper flared as he glared at Reuben, "But we're not done with this, not by a country mile."

REUBEN WENT BACK TO HIS ROAN, MOUNTED UP AND picked up the lead for the mule, although Jack had become accustomed to going with Blue wherever and whenever they started on the move. The lead line was slack as the mule trotted close behind and beside the roan as Reuben went to the head of the wagons to join Asa. As he came near, Asa said, "Ready?"

"Yup, let's move," answered Reuben.

The drivers had been cautioned about the noise, trying to keep their movement as quiet as possible, avoiding the loud whip cracking and shouting that most had become accustomed to, and the only sound was the slap of reins on the rumps of the teams and a spoken command. The wagons stretched out, the usual sounds of trace chains rattling, wheels and axles squealing, and tailgates rubbing and more, the harmony of sounds almost comforting after the noise of battle.

Reuben looked at the sky, dusk settling down over the land, and just a sprinkling of stars that lit their lanterns, but clouds appeared to be gathering in the west, dark and heavy looking. *If we get a storm, it'll be to our advantage, at least for a while, until the trail gets too muddy,* thought Reuben, looking from the clouds and twisting in his saddle to look back at the wagons. He had sent out the outriders, one on each flank, one at the rear, and he rode alone on the point. The young men had proven themselves as outriders, but Reuben had cautioned them to stay alert and stay within sight of the wagons.

The big moon rose golden in the east behind them, shining bright to cast the golden glow on the trail before them. It had started as an almost clear night, but the clouds gathering in the west seemed to be building and Reuben was hopeful of making seven or eight miles before they stopped. They couldn't make much more than that with tired teams that had traveled all day, but with the short rest and the cool night, he was hopeful. The valley of the Platte was bounded north and south by the rolling sandhills of Nebraska territory, sometimes the hills showed juniper and cedar, sometimes they were bald of everything but bunch grass and cacti. Now the hills nearby showed rolling mounds that in the moonlight appeared soft and smooth, even inviting. But appearances can be deceiving, and the cry of coyotes hinted of the hidden dangers that lay within the folds of the hills.

The moon stood high above as it began to slip behind some of the scattered clouds that threatened a storm, and Reuben had noticed the hills on the south were showing flanks of rocky cliffs. He looked to the river, the foliage was spotty, and the distance between the two promised good clearance and a field of fire for the defenders, if necessary. He reined up, stood in his stirrups for a better look around, and satisfied, turned back to the wagons to tell them to start to circle up for the night. He guessed they had covered close to ten miles and was satisfied with the new location.

He reined up, lifted his hand high and gave the

motion to circle up and the lead wagon swung wide to start the circle. Within a few moments, the wagons were in position, and the drivers began unhitching the teams and readying for the night's rest. Reuben rode down the line, speaking to each of the families, "It'd be best if you don't start any fires tonight. Once you're settled, I'll take some men to the trees to get some firewood to put under the wagons in case the storm gets us, but it'd be best just to turn in for some rest." He looked at the men. "Check with your neighbors, take turns standin' watch, two hours each, three men per crew. You choose."

When the movement settled, Reuben made the circle. "I'll lead some to the trees for firewood if you wanna come. But make sure one stays on watch." Five men chose to go with him, and in a short while, all were returning, arms loaded with firewood that was shared with nearby wagons. It was no more than an hour after stopping that silence settled over the wagons and lone sentries could be seen standing or sitting near the ends of wagons, enjoying the still coolness of the night and the random shafts of moonlight that pierced the cloud cover. In the distance, lightning could be seen sending its lances to the ground, followed by the rolling of distant thunder, but the sentries watched as the storm moved across the northern reaches of the hills and passed them by, leaving behind the smells of rainfall and the churning of the disappointed wind.

Twice during the night, Reuben made the rounds of the sentries, encouraging each one to remain vigilant, and looking to the shadows of the trees beside the river. He was pleased with the location of the camp that offered little cover to any attacking enemy and a clear field of fire for the defenders. But he was still restless concerning the Oglala. He also knew they were more than twenty miles from the village, and that distance should be to their advantage, but for a large war party that was already on the move, it would not discourage those intent on retaliation. He breathed heavy, looked to the grey line of early morn, and started his circle of the wagons again.

First light showed several already busy at their wagons, building morning cookfires, checking the gear, greasing axles, and more. Several greeted Reuben as he walked around the circle, but it was Arthur Brown that confronted him. "Am I gonna bury my family here?" he growled, angry at everyone and everything, choosing to take his anger out on Reuben.

"I'll see if I can get a couple men to give you a hand, maybe talk with the pastor, if that'd be alright, Mr. Brown."

"Don't need no help," he growled, dismissively turning away to reach into his wagon for a shovel. He put his rifle and shovel together over his shoulder and started toward the trees by the river.

Reuben continued on his circle, stopping at the wagon of Pastor Wycliffe. "Pastor, Arthur Brown has gone to the trees yonder to start diggin' the graves for his family. You know the people, could you get a couple men to give him a hand, maybe have some ladies tend to the bodies?"

"Certainly, certainly. My wife'll have a couple ladies give her a hand, and I'll get George Betts to help, and we'll spell Arthur."

"Thanks, Pastor," responded Reuben, nodding as he moved away to return to his lone camp. He had made his solitary camp away from the wagons, near a slight depression beside a hump of rocks and brush, but close enough to be aware of all that happened in the circle. He knew there were still several that were suspicious, stand-offish at best, and uncertain about him for he had not been a part of their company. All they knew was he had appeared out of the dark when the captain's men had attempted to take Mabel Betts and her daughter, Made-line, but even that was questionable. As he built his little cookfire, he thought of Elly McGuire and the people of the Mormon train who had readily accepted him, but that was after he had rescued the girls. He smiled as he remembered the blonde Elly, remembering he said he would try to catch up with their train, but now he was burdened with this company. He shook his head, showing his consternation, and pushed the coffee pot closer to the flames.

He had finished his coffee when he saw the pastor approaching, smiling. "Reuben, we'll be havin' a service in a few minutes, in the middle of the wagons, and we'd like you to join us."

"A service? You mean for the burial?"

"No, Arthur just wanted a short service for his family. We already did that, but today is the Lord's day, Sunday, and we're goin' to have church!" he declared, motioning for Reuben to come with him.

Reuben grinned, tossed the dregs of his coffee aside, lay the cup near the pot that now sat away from the coals, and stood to follow the pastor. With his Henry in hand, he was soon beside the pastor. "I ain't been in church since, well, I guess it was 'fore the war!"

"You don't say, well then, it's high time you joined us," laughed the pastor as they neared the others that had already gathered, bringing an assortment of chairs, stools, stumps and more. Reuben went to the back of the small crowd, stood with the butt of his rifle beside his foot and leaning his elbow on his hand at the muzzle. The pastor led the group in a few songs; Rock of Ages and Amazing Grace, the only accompaniment being a pitch pipe, but folks sang out and it was good to hear music instead of gunshots.

When the music ended, the pastor began his message, "I want to use the text from Acts 17:30 *And the times of this ignorance God winked at; but now commandeth all men everywhere to repent.* God doesn't deal in suggestions, he makes commands. We can't help but admit that the times we are livin' in are filled with ignorance. Brother fightin' against brother in the war, red man fightin' white man here in the west, people killin' one another for the poorest of reasons, because we don't agree with one another or because we don't like another. That is what ignorance is, the lack of understandin'.

"We don't want to understand the other man's ways, we want to change them. We don't want to do what someone else says, we want them to do what we say, live like us, be like us. But God made everyone unique. Some tall, some short, some skinny, some, well, fluffy," he smiled as most laughed at his description, "some are red, some white, some brown, some black, all are unique! Because God wanted it that way, He has a marvelous palette of colors for everything! Horses, animals, pigs, goats, cows, and people. Wouldn't the world be borin' if every flower looked and smelled alike? Or every hill, every mountain, every valley, every tree, every river, be the same?"

The pastor was looking at each one, his chin tucked down and looking a little squint-eyed from under his heavy brow, and spoke softly, "You know what I mean, don't you? And what does God say? He says, *repent!* That means 'to turn away' from, but He means even more, He wants you to turn away from the life that is without God. He wants to give you a better life and He offers you the gift of Eternal Life, a life with God in control. Wouldn't it be better to have someone in control that knows what's best? Of course it would!

"Now, here's what each one should do, if you have never done it before. That is to turn away from your previous way of life, accept the gift of eternal life that He offers, just for the askin', and be born again!"

He went on to explain about how the Bible tells us to call upon the name of the Lord, or pray, and ask His forgiveness and ask for the gift that is told about in Romans 6:23 and to do as it says in Romans 10:9-13 and call upon the name of the Lord to be saved. "I will close with I Peter 2:15, *For so is the will of God, that with well doing ye may put to silence the ignorance of foolish men.* You see my friend, once you accept that gift of eternal life and make sure of Heaven as your home, God wants us to live right so that the ignorance will be done away."

He concluded with a prayer, asking God for his blessings, protection, and guidance on the journey ahead. He lifted his eyes to each one and looked to Reuben, "Will we be traveling today, or do we get to rest on this, the Lord's day?"

"That's up to you folks, pastor. I'm just here to help."

As the crowd started to disburse, Arthur Brown, sided by Joshua Becker and Fredrick Hampton, came towards Reuben and he could tell by the look on Brown's face, there was a confrontation coming. Behind them, the pastor also saw the group moving toward Reuben and he stepped away from the others and started in his direction.

Brown was the ringleader and spokesman. "You, what's your name, we wanna talk!" he declared, drawing within arm's reach, thinking to intimidate the younger and slightly smaller Reuben.

Reuben stood his ground, unmoving, and answered somewhat softly, "The name is Reuben, Reuben Grundy, and just what is it you want to talk about, Mr. Brown?"

"First off, nobody elected you to run this train so where do you get off tryin' to take charge?"

"I don't want to take charge, I just wanted to get you out of harm's way, the best I could, and it wasn't the time for discussion or elections."

"Hummph, what's a young pup like you know, anyway?"

"Is that a question?" asked Reuben, frowning.

"What happened with that big wagon and the captain?" growled Brown.

Reuben looked at the other men, wondering if they were backing Brown and were against him for some reason, or if they were just curious. He looked back at Brown, shook his head, "It blew up! I thought you might have heard it," explained Reuben, stepping to the side to sit on a chair brought by the pastor who had seated himself and offered the chair to Reuben.

Reuben sat down and the other men looked about for something to sit on, gathered some stumps, stools and chairs and made themselves as comfortable as possible. Joshua Becker scooted a little closer, glancing from Brown to Reuben, then looked at Reuben as he asked, "But what we want to know is what all happened?"

"You probably remember when you first saw me," began Reuben, laying his Henry across his lap, "and I mentioned the rifles in the back of the big wagon?"

"Yeah," responded Becker, glancing to the others as they nodded agreement.

"He had at least twenty cases of Springfield rifles, but the boxes were marked Bibles and Farm Equipment," he paused and was interrupted by Hampton, "How did you know that?"

"He stopped in Kearny, had the smithy repair his wagon, I helped. And because it was so heavy, we looked to see what the cargo was in case we needed to lighten the load. Our curiosity got the better of us."

"Why didn't you report it to the fort?" asked Becker.

"I did, but the colonel was shippin' out to the war and the new commandant hadn't arrived yet," he chose not to elaborate about the political connections and more. "So, I followed, watched, and listened, suspectin' they were up to no good. I saw the driver meet with the captain and his men, heard enough to be suspicious. And followed. Later, when I saw the Oglala chief meet with the captain and the wagon remain behind, I knew what was about to happen and knew I couldn't let the rifles get in the hands of the Indians."

"So, you blew it up?!" growled Brown.

Reuben just nodded, looking from one man to the other. And Brown stood, fist balled, "Because you blew up the rifles, that's what got the Injuns riled and made 'em attack us and kill my wife an' my boy! I oughta tear you apart!" growled Brown, his anger boiling, his nostrils flaring and the muscles in his jaw flexing as he moved side to side anxiously, ready to strike out, until the pastor stood and stepped between the men, putting his hand on Brown's chest.

"Arthur, settle down. Reuben didn't kill your wife, the Indians did. Reuben warned us to be ready, remember?"

"But if he hadn't made 'em mad, they wouldn't have come after us!" he growled.

"They had attacked the Mormon train the night before, stole five of their women, and that was before any explosion. Think what would have happened yesterday when they attacked this train and if every one of those Oglala warriors were armed with Springfield rifles and plenty of ammunition. It would have been a slaughter and you and your daughter would also be dead!" declared the pastor, glancing from Brown to Reuben and the other men.

"He's right, Art, none of us would be here if they had rifles like that. I only saw a couple with old trade Fusils, most had bows and lances and such. With rifles, I hate to think," added Joshua Becker.

Fredrick Hampton added his agreement, "They're right Art. We should be thankin' him instead of blamin' him. And who was it that kilt those chiefs in the trees?" he asked, looking to Reuben, "Did you do it?"

Reuben nodded, saying nothing.

Hampton, "They was in the trees, over two hundred yards away from us, where were you?"

"On the hill behind the wagons."

All the men looked at Reuben, and Hampton shook his head. "But that's what, five, six hundred yards?"

"More like seven."

The men looked at Reuben, Hampton nodded to the Henry on his lap. "With that?"

Reuben grinned. "No, I used my Sharps."

The men grew quiet, looking at the young man before them who seemed to have aged just in the past couple days, and now grew in their estimation immeasurably.

"Isn't it the far east people that believe if you save a man's life you're forever after responsible for him?" asked Reuben, glancing to the side where Pastor Wycliffe rode with him. The two were out front of the wagons, the second day after the Oglala attack and were enjoying the cool morning and quiet of the land.

The pastor chuckled. "I've heard that, but aren't you thankful that we're not in the far east?"

Reuben laughed. "Indeed I am, Pastor, indeed I am."

"I was encouraged when the people chose Joshua Becker as their captain, he's a good man." The pastor paused, contemplating, "And it was a good idea you had, but I know you were thinkin' of shuckin' the burden of responsibility from your shoulders."

"Well, Pastor, the way I see it, the folks naturally were suspicious of me, an outsider, and bein' younger than most of their men, and most wagon trains elect their leaders from among their number anyway, so it seemed the natural thing to do," he explained as he leaned forward on his pommel, resting one hand on top of the other. "'Sides, a blind man could follow that trail," nodding to the deep ruts in the trail that lay before them. He looked to a nearby bluff to see a small herd of pronghorn antelope grazing in the shade, one lone buck watching them as they passed some three hundred yards away.

"I suppose you'll be wantin' to leave soon and see if you can catch up to the other train, the one with the young lady you spoke about?" asked the pastor, a mischievous smile tugging at the corner of his mouth.

Reuben chuckled. "I only spent a few hours with her and her family, but there was somethin' special about her, right pretty she was."

"It takes a strong woman to walk beside a man in this wild country."

Reuben smiled at the memory of her shooting the Oglala warrior. "She is that. She didn't hesitate to shoot that warrior that tried to take her rifle. Stopped him in a hurry, she did."

"She shot a man?" asked the pastor, incredulous at the thought of a woman shooting down a man.

"One of the bunch that had stolen her and her friends from the wagon train. She wasn't about to be taken again, can't say as I blame her neither."

The pastor looked sidelong at Reuben, asked, "Are you thinkin' of takin' a bride?"

Reuben laughed nervously, twisted a little in his seat and glanced at the pastor. "Oh, I'll admit the thought entered my mind, although I never considered it before, but I think I need to get to know her a little better. Three hours is not much of a courtship, ya' reckon?"

"No, not much, although some have been married with less."

Reuben frowned, shaking his head. "Seems a mite

foolish to make a decision that'll affect the rest of your life on such short acquaintance."

"Oh, I agree, but the times we're livin' in often makes folks do the unexpected."

Reuben pointed to the tree line at the river where several deer were grazing, motioned for the pastor to stop and they both stepped down. Reuben whispered, "You wanna take one?"

The pastor looked at Reuben, back to the deer, and nodded as he slipped his rifle from the scabbard. He had a Spencer 56-56 rimfire, the slug being a .52 caliber. It was a new rifle, usually called a Spencer Repeating rifle and Reuben had yet to see one up close or fire one. The pastor saw Reuben's expression and explained, "I got this just before we left. The merchant said the maker was tryin' to get the Army to buy them, but they were afraid the men would use too much ammunition, so he was sellin' them to anyone that had forty dollars. First time I used it was when the Sioux attacked the wagons."

Reuben nodded, motioned to the deer and suggested, "You take the buck on the right, I'll take the little'r one to the left." He dropped to one knee, using the other to support his elbow and the pastor did the same. "Whenever you're ready," whispered Reuben, already with his sights on his target.

The Spencer barked and spat lead and smoke, echoed by Reuben's Henry that sounded with a lesser bark, almost like a pup compared to the big bulldog. The pastor's buck stumbled and fell, Reuben's took a couple steps, staggered, and dropped on his neck. The others sprang into the brush and could be heard splashing across the water. Reuben looked to the pastor. "Good shot!"

"Surprised?"

"No, well, maybe. Just never thought of a pastor handlin' a rifle, and so well at that."

The pastor smiled, stood and started to the downed deer, glanced at Reuben. "We have to eat too, besides, I wasn't always a pastor. The Bible is clear about our need to *kill and eat*. Throughout the Old Testament and the New, He shows that the bounty of the earth is for our benefit. And He also tells us to fight when necessary, standin' against all evil."

They worked together dressing out the kills and soon had the bundles of meat ready, leaving the entrails and bones behind for the already circling turkey buzzards and other carrion eaters. They moved away to the shade of a pair of tall sycamore, and Reuben looked at the pastor. "Pastor, would you stay here and wait for the wagons? This looks like a likely place to take the noonin' and you could hand off the meat as you see fit. I think I'm gonna let Blue stretch his legs a mite and see if we can't catch up with that other train."

"You mean catch up with that girl, don'tchu?" asked the pastor, grinning.

Reuben ducked his head, the blush climbing his neck as he chuckled a little, then looked up at the pastor. "Pastor, I'm like George Washington, I cannot tell a lie. Yes, you are right, it is that blonde haired girl that's got me a little bamboozled."

The pastor laughed, nodding. "I understand. You go ahead, I'll wait for the wagons."

"I might be waiting further up the trail, dependin'..."

"Dependin' on her, or on her father?"

Reuben laughed. "Both."

———

HE LET BLUE HAVE HIS HEAD AND THE BIG ROAN stretched out, not to be outdone by Jack the pack mule who kept pace close beside. It was a fast walk, and both were eager to make time. It was late afternoon before they stopped and had a short rest, time enough for Reuben to brew a pot of coffee and down some jerky and the animals to crop some grass and have a good drink of fresh water from the little rivulet that came from the hills. He knew the moon would be waning from full and it would be a cool night to travel, so he chose to give the animals ample rest and to take a short snooze himself before traveling further.

It was but a couple hours before Blue nudged Reuben awake, lifted his head to look down the tree line, ears pricked and eyes wide. Reuben rolled to the side, came to his feet, Henry in hand, to see a small band of natives moving across the flat toward the river, less than a mile upstream from where he stood. He guessed there to be about fifteen, most mounted, but a few walking beside the several travois laden horses. There were women and children and best he could tell, the men were not painted for war, but a little paint never kept a warrior from counting coup or taking a scalp.

He stood unmoving, his free hand resting on the withers of Blue, as they watched the band move to the trees. As late as it was, he wondered if they would be making camp beside the river, and if so, how would he make it past them? He watched as they moved, wondering if they were Oglala or some other band or tribe. He glanced back at the stack of gear, the packs with trade goods, and decided to take a risk, maybe make a trade and some friends.

The sun was lowering in the west, and he rode into the brightness, shading his eyes with the brim of his hat, but watching the tree line where the band had entered. The cluster of trees was thick, but trails were evident, and the recent passage of the many riders showed where they entered the woods. As he neared the tracks, he reined up, sat silent and still, watching, listening, and waiting. He lifted his right hand, palm open and forward, and spoke in a normal tone, "I come in peace to trade. I have trade goods for you." He lowered his hand and repeated himself as best he could using sign language and repeating the words.

Two men showed themselves, one with a bow and nocked arrow, but he held it low as they looked at Reuben. He repeated his offer to trade, and the men motioned him to step down. When he stood beside the roan, one of the men motioned him to go to the trail ahead of him, and Reuben complied. As he entered the clearing, he saw the people busy at making their meal and preparing their brush shelters for the night. Most stopped and stared as he entered, until one of the warriors came beside him and spoke to the others. When he stopped speaking, two older men came forward and the older one, a man that appeared to be in his late forties, a touch of grey in his long black braids and wearing a fringed tunic over his buckskin leggings, two feathers dangling from the back of his hair. He frowned at Reuben, came nearer, and looked at the horse and mule, then back to Reuben. "You trade?"

"Yes, I've come to trade. My goods are in the packs on the mule."

The man turned to the one beside him, spoke an order and the man went quickly to a stack of gear, fetched a blanket, and returned, laying the blanket out for the men to be seated. The older man motioned for Reuben to get his goods, and Reuben nodded, dropping the rein of the blue to ground tie him, walked back to the mule and stripped off the pack of trade goods, grabbed a blanket and returned to the space before the men. He stretched out the blanket and began to display his wares, knives, hatchets, beads, vermillion, and more. One pack of sugar sat to the side, a bag of cornmeal and one of flour beside it. Reuben had been on his knees arranging the trade goods, motioned to the men and they began looking and examining.

As the women began sorting through the goods, Reuben introduced himself, using sign as well as English. "I am Reuben Grundy, a trader passing through on the way to Fort Laramie."

The obvious leader nodded, and spoke using sign, but also surprised Reuben as he spoke in English. "I am Tatánka Wakan, Medicine Bull, of the Sičháŋǧu Oyáte Lakota, some call us Brule. We have come from a buffalo hunt, return to our village to the north."

"Did you have a good hunt?" asked Reuben, casually watching the women examining the goods.

"It was a good hunt. The buffalo move," he motioned with his hand to the west and north, "in a big herd, all day to pass."

"Perhaps I will find them, take some meat for myself, but with so much, unless there are others to share, I will not kill one."

"This is good. Many white men kill, take only the hide, leave rest for buzzards and coyotes. My people go hungry."

Reuben shook his head. "It is wrong that they do this."

The chief nodded, looked at the women who had made their choices and were ready to trade. He looked at Reuben, "What do you want?" motioning to the goods.

"Well, I need a set or two of buckskins, britches, shirt, moccasins. Maybe a good bow and some arrows."

The chief frowned. "You try to be Indian?"

Reuben grinned. "No," and grabbed at his shirt, "No good, wears out."

The chief nodded, translated to the women and two women left, as the others waited, handfuls of beads, needles, bells, mirrors and more. When the two returned, they laid out a complete set of newly finished, beaded, and fringed buckskins and a pair of moccasins. Reuben stood, held the items next to him, judged them to be a reasonable fit, tried on the moccasins and nodded. After the trades were completed, he had two sets of buckskins, but no bow and arrows, but he was pleased with his trade. He gave the chief a special knife that he had held back, similar to a Bowie but not as big, yet it was well made with an antler handle, brass haft, and sharp blade. The chief's eyes grew wide as he examined the blade and more, looked up as Reuben explained, "That is a gift for you for allowin' me to trade with your people. I hope we will be friends, perhaps I will pass this way again."

The chief nodded, motioned to one of the women, and watched as Reuben packed up the rest of the goods, and readied to leave. The woman returned with a small bundle which she handed to him. He accepted the bundle, frowning, then turned to the man, who was now standing, and offered his hand to shake. The chief nodded, explaining, "That is meat from the buffalo, now you do not have to kill one," and eagerly shook hands with the young man, said simply, "Friend," and stepped back. Reuben mounted up, reined around, and rode from the trees, turning the blue roan to the west and into the fading light of dusk. He had a long ride before him, but he was getting anxious to see Elly and spend some time with her. He had learned much from the chief of the Brule, Medicine Bull, and hoped they would meet again. It was the first time he had made friends with any of the natives, and he was pleased with himself but knew he would need to resupply on his trade goods if he intended to do much more, but for now, he was more intent on a different kind of friendship.

"There are three building blocks to the making of a man," began Micah Grundy, speaking to his three sons. They were taking a short break on their hunting trip into the woods around White Pigeon, Michigan territory, and had sat on a couple of logs that had fallen in a blow down a few years prior. The father of the brood often took advantage of any opportunity to teach his sons what he believed they needed to know as they grew into manhood. He continued, "The first of these is morality, that's the gaining the knowledge of right and wrong, and knowing that those morals are like the frame of building a home. Morals are the difference between good and evil. For example, morals are your compass for the direction of your life – if you know something is not good or right, you avoid it. But that which is good, you always seek to do what's right."

"What's the second building block, Pa?" asked the youngest of the three, Raphael, who had just turned twelve and was curious about all things about becoming a man.

"Well, the second is Character. Character is what you

are because of your choices, those choices of right and wrong that make you a man, or something less. A man with character will be a man of his word, and seek to do right to and for others, even when those others make the wrong choices, and character is never compromised." He looked into the faces of his sons, each one making him proud of the men they were becoming. His oldest, Rufus, would probably become a farmer like his father, the second, Reuben, was more adventurous and had not shown what he would become, and the youngest, Raphael, always curious, but loyal and a homebody, had yet to experience much of life to show any direction to his life.

"And the third, is Faith. That's where you stand with God. And that will become the most important block of your life for that will influence every choice, every decision, everything in your life. That's why I've left much of that teaching to your mother, she's a little more spiritual than I am and much more compassionate, so she's better at teaching you about those things. Although I depend upon God every day of my life and I know Jesus as my Savior, that's a decision each of you must make, and I pray you make the right one."

REUBEN ROCKED IN HIS SADDLE WITH THE EASY GAIT OF HIS blue roan, trailing the pack mule, and wistfully remembered the words of his father. It seemed like it had been yesterday when they made that hunt in the woods by their farm, yet it was also an eternity ago when they separated; Rufus, the first to join the Union forces, then Reuben, while Raphael stayed to home with the folks. And now he was the only one of the three brothers left. He let a heavy sigh lift his shoulders and bring his attention back to the present, and he scanned the valley bottom in the early morning light. He had been riding most of the night, using the waning moon as his guiding light, keeping it off his left shoulder for most of the early morning hours.

He had been keeping to the west edge of the long river bottomed valley, avoiding the more obvious route beside the wagon road and the timber laden riverbank. Always careful to have cover accessible, he watched the grey sky slowly fading to pale blue as the sun bent its golden shafts over the eastern horizon and brought the hint of warmth to the valley that was showing the green of spring. Movement near the river caught his attention and he watched as a handful of deer, probably six or eight, as they rose from their beds in the tall grasses to make their way to the river's edge. He smiled as he saw some spindly legged fawns trying to keep up with their mothers, then turned his attention to the wagon tracks and the valley to the northwest as the North Platte carved its way between the low rising and sparsely covered hills of Nebraska territory.

He was hopeful of catching up with the Mormon wagon train, eager to see the smiling face of Elly and her bouncing blonde curls, dimpled cheeks, and the mischievous light in her blue eyes. He shook his head and smiled as he thought of the girl, still uncertain of his feelings and thoughts about the future, after all, he had nothing to offer a woman that he might ask to be his wife, his life's partner. What woman would want to have nothing but the back of a horse for a home? *What am I thinking about a wife for? She won't want to leave her family, especially since you don't have anything to offer! What's the matter with you? Maybe you should just turn around and make yourself scarce, that'd prob'ly be the best for both of you!*

"Well! It's about time! I'd almost given up on you!" came a voice from the edge of the cluster of junipers at the flank of the hill beside him. Reuben was startled and reined up to look into the face of Elly as she sat astride the bay mare of her father, smiling broadly and laughing at his surprise.

"What...?" stuttered Reuben, looking around and past the girl, searching for the wagon train. "What are you doin' here, alone!? Don't you know there's Indians about? And who knows what all!"

Elly laughed. "Aren't you glad to see me?"

Reuben shook his head, laughing. "Happier to see you than the risin' sun!" he declared, swinging down from Blue and reaching up to help her down. She accepted his offered hands, swung her leg over of the pommel and slid into his arms, standing close and looking up into his whiskered face.

"Don't just stand there, kiss me!" she declared and stretched to her tiptoes.

Reuben willingly complied, holding her close and covering her lips with his, pulled back to look at her and wrapped her in a hug and embrace. They moved apart to look at one another, both smiling broadly and letting their presence and happiness speak for them.

Reuben stuttered again, "I, uh, I tried to get away sooner, but..."

"Never mind that, you're here now and that's all that matters to me. I rode out every evening and every morning, looking for you and when you didn't come, I was so afraid you didn't want to, then I was afraid something happened."

Reuben motioned her to a big rock as he dropped the reins to the roan to ground tie him and followed her to the flat stone. They sat close beside one another as she reached for his hand to hold between hers. "What does your dad think about you ridin' out by yourself?"

She smiled. "He knew he couldn't stop me, and momma tried to explain to him about love and girls and boys." She giggled as she watched him squirm on the rock. "What's the matter, you nervous about something?"

Reuben shook his head. "I dunno. I mean, I want to be with you, but..."

"But what? Don't you know how I feel?"

"That's just it, it's more than feelin's. We hardly know each other, but I can't stop thinkin' about you, and I don't want to!" stammered Reuben. "But, I don't have anythin' to offer, no home, no...well, nothin' that would make any woman want to be with a man."

Elly smiled. "So, you have been thinking like I have, about being husband and wife?"

The color rose up Reuben's neck and he felt the heat of embarrassment. "Yeah, I have," and he hastened to add, "But I've never thought that way about anyone before!"

"Me neither. But when I think about you, I just want to be with you, no matter what!"

"But, Elly, I don't even know where I'm goin' to be, where I'm goin' to go! I only trailed after the wagons cuz o' the gunrunners and knew somethin' had to be done about them. But that's over, and I dunno, maybe I could go on to Fort Laramie, or..." He stubbed his toe in the dirt, looked up at her and added, "I talked to a fella back at Kearny that said the freight wagons goin' to Santa Fe could use a man like me to hunt and provide meat for the mule skinners, and there's always work on the wagon trains for scouts and such. Another fella said he was workin' for the stage line, and they always needed

211

messengers or shotgunners and drivers. But ain't no place for a woman!"

"I can ride a horse as good as any man, and I can shoot a rifle or a pistol as good as any man! Whatever you do, I can do! Wherever you go, I can go!" She had slid from the rock and stood before him, hands on her hips, feet apart, and it was the first he noticed she was wearing buckskin britches not unlike his own.

Reuben turned toward her, looking at the deep-set blue eyes and the determination that blazed from them. Her expression was stoic, and her resolve was written not just on her countenance but her very stance appeared unmovable and her commitment unshakeable.

"Do you love me?" she asked, as she relaxed and moved her hands from her hips to his shoulders, stepping close to him.

"I think so, uh," he stammered, looking into her eyes. "Yeah, I do! I don't understand it, but, yeah, I do!" he said, more resolutely as he pulled her closer still.

She smiled, leaned forward, and kissed him, then leaned back a smidge. "That's all I wanted to hear, because I love you too!" she declared. She giggled a little, tried to look serious and said, "You look hungry! You got anything to eat in those packs?" nodding toward the mule.

"Uh, yeah, there's some fresh buffalo meat in that bundle atop there, and some other stuff in the parfleche behind it."

"Good, get a fire going and I'll fix us breakfast while you go to the creek yonder and wash up and shave. If you expect to be loving on me, I don't need no whisker burns to explain to papa 'fore we get hitched!"

The herd was moving with the first light of day. Although the mass of brown wooly bodies traveled at a walking gait, the lumbering buffalo made the ground move as thousands of the massive beasts beat the spring growth of grass into submission with their ponderous hooves. The wagon train had made camp near the river and in the open just below the crest of the rolling hills that sided the valley, and now the brown blanket smothered the valley, muddied the waters, and churned the soil, making the Mormon families fearful of the near passing beasts.

The rolling rumble of their passing was like muted thunder, as if every footfall moved the earth beneath them, and the ground shook as they moved. The roar was the discordant bellows of the bulls, the bleating of the calves, and the moans of the cows sounding as the inharmonious choir of the plains. A heavy cloud of dust rose from both their hooves and the heavy wool of their coats that carried the remains of many dust baths taken by the bulls to dull the bites of parasites. Cowbirds rode atop the humps, picking at the fleas, ticks, and more that were hitchhiking a free ride and taking a free meal.

Hurriedly, the many families of the wagon train hitched up the oxen and mules to move the wagons further up the low rise to provide a barrier of distance for safety. The herd was so massive it was immediately evident it would take most of the day, or more, to pass. The wagons were moving up the hillside when Reuben and Elly crested the hill to see the commotion and watch as everyone scurried about. Reuben stood in his stirrups and shaded his eyes as he looked to the hills on the south side of the valley, where the herd was erupting from a low swale and wide basin between the low buttes. But it was not the herd he focused on, rather a group of riders that he recognized as a band of natives. He remembered what Bridger had told him about the Arapaho and that their land was mostly south of the North Platte River and that they were usually friendly to the whites, often seeking to trade with passing wagons.

He turned to Elly who was watching the wagons, looking for her family and said, "There's a huntin' party of natives, probably Arapaho, on the flanks of that herd. We better get down to the wagons and find the wagon master and let him know."

Elly turned wide-eyed to Reuben, prompting him to point out the band far to the south, barely visible and hardly noticeable at this distance, but she saw them and looked back at Reuben. "Will they come after the wagons?"

"Probably not. I reckon they're just huntin' meat and will be busy with the herd. It's usually an all-day affair and involves the whole village. But no tellin' what they'll think if the people from the wagons start shootin' the beasts."

"They wouldn't do that, would they?"

Reuben again stood in his stirrups, nodded, and pointed to the shoulder from the hill where three men were taking position among some rocks, rifles in hand. "*They* might." He turned back to Elly, "You go find the wagon master or your father. I'll go down there where those men are and see if I can put a stop to it."

Without an answer, Elly dug her heels into the bay's ribs and launched them off the hilltop, bound for the wagons. Reuben shifted his weight forward, clenched his knees, and Blue quickly stepped out, pulling the mule's lead line taut, and they started across the crest of the hill to drop down nearer the men. Before he neared, he heard the dull blast of the rifles, knowing the men were already starting their assault on the herd. He kicked the roan to a canter as they charged down the hill and slid to a stop behind the men. The sudden moves from behind startled the men and two of the three rose to their feet and turned to face Reuben as he swung to the ground.

"What do you think you're doin'?" demanded Reuben, glaring at the men.

"What business is it of your'n?" asked the bigger of the three, starting to raise his Spencer toward the intruder.

Reuben noticed the move, held his left hand out toward the man. "You lift that rifle any further and it'll be the last thing you do!" as he slipped his Remington revolver from the holster at his left hip, bringing it to bear on the startled man. A moment of frozen silence stopped the men, eyes widening at the sudden move of Reuben, until he slowly lifted his arm to point to the south. "There's about sixty or seventy Arapaho warriors startin' their hunt on this herd and if you interfere, they will be more than happy to use their weapons on you and your families back at the wagons!"

The men turned to look where he pointed, shaded their eyes as they frowned, staring through the dust. One man said, "I don't see nuthin'!"

"Me neither," responded another.

"What'chu tryin' to pull, mister? We was just havin' a little sport!" added the big man.

"Yeah! There's thousan's of 'em, what's a few more or less with so many?" choked the second man, coughing on the dust of the herd.

"The natives see these as their lifeline. They depend on them for everything, food, shelter, and more. Most consider them sacred even, and to kill just for sport is a waste and an insult to the entire tribe!" Reuben shook his head at what he considered wanton waste and utter stupidity of the men, then added, "You best plan on dressin' out your kills and usin' the meat and more, because if you leave them to rot, those warriors back there will probably come lookin' for you to add your carcass to the pile!" He turned away and grabbed up the rein of Blue, stuck his foot in the stirrup and stepped aboard. He looked down at the men as two of them mumbled to one another, as Reuben warned, "But, you're grown men, so you just do whatever you think is right." He reined Blue around, snatched at the lead of the mule, and started back to the wagons.

The herd continued to rumble past, and the cries of the Arapaho warriors drifted toward him as he nudged the roan to the wagons that were now circling in a low basin that sat almost atop the butte. He saw Elly, still atop her bay as she sat beside a wagon, leaning over the pommel of her saddle talking to her mother beside the wagon. He nudged Blue that direction, taking a deep breath to strengthen his resolve, unknowing as to what to expect from Elly's parents.

He reined up beside Elly, swung his leg over Blue's rump and stepped to the ground. He walked around to the side of Elly's bay, reached up his hands to help her down and gently lowered her to the ground. Although Elly's mother tried not to notice, it was evident she was watching Reuben's attentions to her daughter. Reuben walked back to the mule and lifted off the bundle of bison meat, handed it to Elly's mother, Abigail, and explained, "That was a gift from Tatánka Wakan, Medicine Bull, of the Sičháŋǧu Oyáte Lakota. He's their chief and we made a little trade. If you've never had buffalo meat, I'm sure you'll find it quite tasty."

"Why thank you, Reuben. That's very thoughtful of you. My husband will be back shortly. Elly sent him after the wagon master." She rolled her eyes as if the errand was unwarranted but tolerated.

"Good, good. I've something I need to explain to Mr. Stenhouse," answered Reuben, glancing around to see the two men approaching.

"So good to see you again Reuben. What brings you back to our wagons?" and with a grin toward Elly, "As if I didn't know."

Reuben dropped his gaze to the ground at his suggestion but lifted his eyes again to face the wagon master. He glanced to the south side of the valley. "You've got company," pointing with his chin toward the band of Arapaho warriors. "I think they're Arapaho, but not sure. If they are, they're usually friendly, at least that's what Jim Bridger told me, but it's best to be wary anyway."

"What's this about some of our men shooting buffalo?" asked Stenhouse.

"There were three of them 'havin' a little sport' by

217

shootin' a bunch of buffalo. I cautioned them against it because of the Arapaho and the common sense of it, but whether or not they'll listen, well..." answered Reuben.

"Well, with that herd numbering in the thousands, what's a few more or less?" asked the wagon master.

"If you have to ask, I can't tell you. Other than to caution you regardin' the natives. As you probably know, they see the buffalo as sacred. They depend on the buffalo for just about everythin' in their life, food, lodgin', clothin', tools. And the idea of killin' an animal for sport is somethin' they don't understand, and frankly, neither do I." He paused, looking at the man to judge his reaction, and continued, "But I suggested those three men dress out the animals they killed, put the meat to use, and maybe the Arapaho would understand, but..." he shrugged his shoulders as he looked back to the leader of the wagons.

"I see your point. Perhaps it would be best not to rile the natives. I'm not anxious to have another set-to with any of them."

"Well, I'm sure if you waited a spell for their hunt to taper off, maybe some of your men could take some buffalo for meat, but it's quite a job to dress them out!" declared Reuben, shaking his head.

The wagon master nodded, glancing from Reuben to Jerome and Abigail, Elly's parents, then turned away, but paused and looked back at Reuben. "Thank you for your advice, it's not often that a young man like you has anything to say that I'd be willing to heed, but you've been a help to us twice now. If you'd be interested, I could use a good scout and meat hunter for the wagons the rest of the way to the promised land."

"Thanks for the offer, Mr. Stenhouse, but if I'm to scout for wagons, there's a train that will probably be showin' up any time now that I've already been helpin'." The wagon master waved over his shoulder as he strode off to speak to the other men and pass on the words of caution. Reuben turned toward Elly, but noticed her father looking at her mother with raised eyebrows and wide eyes and wondered what silent messages they were sharing as many married couples did with nothing more than a look or a glance.

Abigail stepped next to Elly, looked at Reuben. "Reuben, would you join us for our midday meal?"

"I'd be happy to, Mrs. McGuire. Is there anythin' I can add that would be of help to you?"

"Just your company, Reuben. That's all we ask," she answered, with another glance to her husband that raised Reuben's curiosity and concern.

"I'm goin' to go see the Arapaho, maybe do a little tradin' with 'em while they're busy with the butcherin' and such," explained Reuben as he tightened the girth on Blue. It was late afternoon and most of the herd had passed them by, with the usual stragglers lagging behind.

"But isn't that dangerous?" asked Elly.

"Maybe, but if I can make peace with 'em, they won't come after the wagons, so, it should be worth it."

"Then I'm coming with you!" declared Elly.

Reuben stopped and stared at the girl, astounded that she would make such a declaration knowing the possible danger she would be going into, yet showing a determination that sanctioned no argument. He turned to her father with an expression of *do something*, but he shrugged and shook his head. Reuben looked at Abigail for some reprieve, but she turned away. He looked back at Elly who was already mounting the bay, her back to him and leaving him no recourse but to allow what she was committed to by her actions. He walked to Blue, stroked his head and quietly asked his four-footed friend, "Are you sure we're up to this?" and swung aboard.

They rode the shoulder of the low rising hills, staying above any stragglers of the herd and going to the south end of the churned-up valley where the Arapaho were beginning the butchering of the downed beasts. The wide swath of trodden and turned soil lay like a fresh tilled farmer's field, leaving a trail that crossed the valley and climbed the dry hills to disappear over the rise to the northwest. Reuben reined up, motioning Elly beside him and they sat overlooking the killing field where as many as forty carcasses lay with people gathering around them already busy at their work. Overhead turkey buzzards, ravens, and eagles circled and below, the carrion eaters were already drawing near; coyotes, badgers, bobcats, and more would soon be fighting for every scrap, overcoming their natural aversion to people to sneak in for a morsel.

Each carcass had two or more women and a few men at work. Although considered women's work, the men were needed to use their horses or manpower to roll the carcass over and off the hide. Horses with travois stood nearby and would soon be laden with meat, hides and even bones, to trail back to the village. Yet some were already starting cookfires for the evening feast on fresh meat and the celebration of a successful hunt that would provide for the people for months to come.

Elly sat mesmerized as she watched the women at work, shaking her head. "So the men just watch while the women do all the work?"

Reuben chuckled. "See what you're gettin' yourself into?"

"Now wait just a minute! If you think we're gonna be living like the Indians, you're greatly mistaken! I will work alongside you, and do everything properly expected of a loving wife, but we do things together!"

Reuben chuckled. "Ummhmm, just what I thought, already making conditions!" and grinned at Elly as he shrugged. "Come on, let's go down there."

"Uh, somebody's coming!" she declared as she pointed to the edge of the valley to a small group of warriors that had spotted them and were charging up the low rise toward them, waving lances and shouting.

"Just sit still and keep your hands away from any weapons," replied Reuben.

"Weapons!? I don't have any weapons!" she answered, watching the approach of the Arapaho.

There were four men that charged toward the two intruders and as they neared, they split with two going to the side of each rider. One of the men shouted at Reuben in the tongue of the Arapaho, gesturing with his lance until Reuben started using sign language. With the sign and English, he said they had come in peace and to trade with the Arapaho people. He motioned to the mule with the packs and added that he had many goods to trade.

One of the men beside Elly reached out to touch her hair and she forced herself to sit still, but when he pulled on her hair, she slapped his hand away and shouted, "NO!"

The warrior jerked away, startled at her response, and frowned, growling something in his own language that elicited the laughter of the man beside him who added some remark that apparently said something about his fear of the woman, making the others laugh as well. The laughter broke the mood of anger and the apparent leader signed back to Reuben, "Follow us to trade with the people."

They were led to a large group that had gathered near a cluster of cottonwoods that grew near a small seep. A dignified man, broad shouldered and deep chested with a stoic expression stood with arms folded across his chest and glaring at the intruders. The leader of the four that brought Reuben and Elly to them spoke, gesturing to the pair, and the man, apparently the chief or leader stepped forward. "I am Little Raven, chief of the *Hinono'eino,* the Arapaho people." He pointed with his chin to the previous speaker, "Red Pipe says you have come to trade."

"I am Reuben Grundy, and this is my woman, Elly. Yes, we have come to trade with your people."

"Are you with the wagons?" asked the chief, nodding toward the encampment of the wagons.

"Yes. We have come in peace and to ask for your permission to take some buffalo for meat."

"We will speak of this." He motioned to the edge of the trees where a grassy flat extended toward the seep. "You can put your blanket there. My people will come to see your goods. What is it you wish to trade for?"

"Perhaps some buckskins," he plucked at his buckskin britches, "for my woman. Maybe some tanned hides or..." and shrugged his shoulders to indicate most anything for trade.

"My people will tell others, they will come as they can," offered the chief. He watched as Reuben and Elly spread out the trade goods on the blanket. With no opportunity to re-supply, his goods had not changed. He spread out awls, knives, pins, needles, verdigris, vermillion, small mirrors, combs, buttons, blue and white beads and several axes and metal tomahawks. But because of the successful hunt, he knew there would be interest in a couple of items he had saved back from the Brule, a cast iron Dutch oven and a copper-bottomed pot, both prized items among the natives.

The chief stood to the side but kept watching as the display grew and his eyes shone bright when he spotted a hatchet with a pipe bowl on one end and the metal blade on the other. He came close and bent to pick up the hatchet, hefted it and swung it to get the feel of the weapon, grinned and asked, "What will you trade for this?"

Reuben looked up at Little Raven, noticed his necklace and motioned to it so the chief would let him look at it. It was a four layered hair pipe bone necklace with stones and beads between each piece of bone, but what caught Reuben's eye was the center stones. When the chief handed it to him, he carefully examined the different stones, several were turquoise, a few were carved red soapstone, but in the center, two of the four stones were gold nuggets. Reuben looked carefully at the larger-than-thumbnail sized nuggets, and back to the chief. With a quick glance to his wares, Reuben picked up a Green River knife, and a handful of other goods, beads, needles and more, and handed it all to the chief. "The hatchet and these for the necklace."

The chief looked at Reuben, frowned and looked at the goods. "But I just want the hatchet."

"The necklace is worth more than the hatchet. The knife and the rest with the hatchet is a good trade," answered Reuben.

The chief smiled, nodded. "You are a good man. It is a good trade."

In just a short while, several others made their way to the trade site, looking over the goods and returning with items to trade. Two women, after looking at the goods, looked at Elly and spoke to one another, gesturing to Elly. The chief stood to the side, but watched, and chuckled at the women. He spoke up so Elly could hear and said, "They are saying your hair is like the meadowlark, gold like the sun."

Elly self-consciously touched her hair and smiled at the women, then spoke to the chief, "They were also looking at the pots. If they have a dress like what they have, and some leggings that would fit me, we will consider trading the pot for them."

The chief smiled, nodded, and translated Elly's words to the women who excitedly chattered to one another, and trotted off, motioning they would return. The women soon returned, somewhat dejected, and with the chief translating, they explained they did not have the items with them but did have more back at their village. Elly rose and went closer to the chief and the women and the four spoke together, as Reuben tried to listen but was busy with other trades.

Elly returned, smiling broadly, and said, "I'm going with the women to get the dress and such from their village. They said we will be back before full dark, so wait for me and don't trade those pots."

"I don't want you going off by yourself. Anything could happen! No, you stay here."

Elly smiled, and answered, "Just wait for me, please?"

Reuben shook his head, motioned to those still looking to trade, and stood to go to Blue. The horses and mule had been tethered to the trees near the grass and he unstrapped the scabbard with the Henry rifle and hung it under the right fender of Elly's saddle. He knew it was fully loaded and that she knew how to handle it, but it was little consolation for what she was determined to do and go with the other women. But he knew an argument would be useless.

She had watched him hang the scabbard and smiled when he returned. "I know, I know, be careful. I will and I'm certain there is no danger. These are good women." She tightened the girth on the bay and stepped aboard, reined him around and bent down to kiss Reuben. She sat up, smiling and nudged the bay away to join the two women on her excursion back to their village.

Although she was unfamiliar with sign language, she had watched Reuben and with some signing, mostly just gesturing and speaking as women do, the trio seemed to make one another understand. The conversation with the chief had covered most of what they needed to know, and they enjoyed trying to communicate, mostly laughing and struggling to understand, but somehow the universal language of friendship seemed to prevail.

REUBEN HAD FINISHED PACKING UP THE REMAINS OF HIS trade goods and sat talking with Little Raven about the ways of the Arapaho people and the recent events in the west. Little Raven told of going with Niwot, his friend, and another chief of the Arapaho, to Denver to see what all the hubbub was about with the gold strike. "I told the men that were digging in the ground for the yellow stone that we are friends but that I hoped they would soon find all the stones and go back where they came from, but I do not think they will leave." He chuckled as he looked at Reuben. "I know that is why you like my necklace, the yellow stones do things to the white people."

Reuben chuckled. "Yes, you are right about that, Little Raven. There are some men that would do anythin' for the yellow stone. I don't understand it either, but that is the way with many men. Is it not so with your people? Perhaps it is for horses or women or some other thing that your people value that some men want so badly they will even kill for it?"

"That is true. But when you grow old," he touched the grey streak in his hair, "like me, you learn that other things mean more than yellow stones or many horses. It is better to have a good woman, a warm lodge, and children around you that give you warmth," he patted his chest with his open hand, "here." He looked at Reuben, smiled. "The woman with yellow hair will be a good wife for you. She is strong and a good warrior to walk beside you."

Reuben frowned. "Did she say she was goin' to be my wife?"

Little Raven smiled. "Yes, but I could see that before she spoke. You two are like this," he cupped the fingers of both hands and brought them together like coupled links, "stronger together than apart."

Reuben looked up at the sound of approaching horses and was relieved to see the three women returning, smiling, and laughing with one another. Elly reined up and looked at Reuben. "Did you save out the pots for me?"

He nodded to the two pots that sat beside the panniers that were yet to be loaded onto the pack mule. She smiled and stepped down, picked up both pots and handed one to one to each woman. "Thank you! This has been a wonderful day and I hope to see you again!"

The chief spoke up and translated, although he thought the women already understood what was meant even though they did not understand the words. The women chattered, nodded, and smiled to Elly, and

227

turned their mounts away to go back to their work with the other women and probably to show off their new pots.

Elly smiled to Reuben. "You ready to go back to the wagons, or are we staying?"

Reuben shook his head. "I think we best go back. Your father would not be too happy with me if I didn't bring you back safely."

As they started away from the Arapaho camp, Reuben said, "Well, you're not wearin' anything new, so what'd you get for my pots?"

Elly smiled and said, "Something special!" but did not explain as she kicked the bay to a canter, anxious to get back to her mother and sister. Reuben shook his head and followed, wondering just what he was going to do about this girl.

The white tops of the wagons swayed in rhythm with one another as they bounced along the rutted wagon tracks of the thousands that had gone before. Reuben watched from atop the hill where he made his camp above the wagons of the Mormon train. He sat in the shade of the scraggly cedar, pondering the coming day and the events it promised. Remembering his talk with Elly's dad, Jerome, he considered the man's counsel. "Reuben, the two of you are doing what you believe is right and what your hearts are telling you, but I must say, I have my reservations. Just what do you plan to do? And what kind of a home are you going to give my daughter?"

"Honestly, Mr. McGuire, I don't know. We've talked about it and about the only thing we've settled on is goin' south to Julesburg and maybe gettin' on with the Butterfield stage line. Elly's determined to stay by my side no matter what we decide, and as far as a home..." he waved his arms around them, "this is all I have to offer. But I promise you this, your daughter will never want for love or anythin' else of value. I will protect her with my life and provide for her before myself."

The older man dropped his eyes, shaking his head, and looked up at Reuben. "I admit I am concerned for my daughter, but I can't help but remember the time her mother and I made the same choice you're making. I had no job, no prospects, and only twenty dollars in my pocket when we ran off and got married. Both my folks and hers were livid and anxious, but when they got over it, we had one tremendous party for the whole settlement." He chuckled at the memory, "But don't you say anything to her mother about this. Now, you're gonna have your hands full with that headstrong girl, but I think you can handle it. Even though she most often acts like she's a boy, that one is all woman; and you are a mighty lucky man. You take care of her, or I'll come looking for you! Got that?" declared the man, looking sternly at Reuben.

"Yessir, I will sir!" answered Reuben.

At the recollection of the conversation, Reuben shook his head, *I hope you know what you're doin'!* He was a little nervous, maybe apprehensive, at what was about to happen, but the very thought of the blue-eyed blonde with the mischievous smile brought a smile to his face and butterflies to his stomach.

He looked around the terrain and was surprised to see a small group of Arapaho coming toward the wagons. As near as he could make out there were six riders plus an additional horse pulling a laden travois. Reuben frowned, curious as to the visit but certain it was friendly. He stood and walked down the slope, leaving his animals picketed in the shade of the junipers and with ample grass for graze.

As the Arapaho neared, he recognized Little Raven

and his woman, Red Bear. The two women that had befriended Elly rode together and led the horse with the travois. Two other warriors sided Little Raven and Reuben recognized them as two of those that first met him the day before. With his hand raised high, palm forward, Reuben greeted them, "Yah te hay, Little Raven."

"hii3eti'nohkuseic/Nii'ooke', good morning," replied the chief. He motioned to the two men, "This is Red Pipe and Black Nose, we will help you prepare for the ceremony." He motioned to the women. "They are Running Antelope and Wind in her Hair, they will help my woman and they will help Meadowlark prepare for the ceremony."

Reuben frowned. "Ceremony?"

Little Raven chuckled. "Your joining! Has not the woman, Meadowlark, told you?"

Reuben slowly lifted his head, letting a slow smile split his face. "Do the women tell us anything?"

Reuben motioned for them to step down just as she heard Elly call, "Running Antelope, Wind in her Hair! You came!" He turned to see Elly quickstepping it toward them, her mother and sister following close behind. Red Bear had stepped down with the women and smiled as Elly came near, translating for the two younger women. She had learned English with her husband and Reuben would later learn the woman was fluent in many languages, both of the natives and the white men. Elly ignored Reuben as she introduced her mother and sister and the women quickly moved away, leading the horses including the one with the travois.

Little Raven grinned at Reuben. "Do not worry my friend, the women will do what is needed." He glanced to the men, motioned to them and they took the horses and moved away. Little Raven put his arm around the shoulders of Reuben. "I know you will want to have your holy man speak his words at your ceremony, what we will do is prepare you and your woman for that ceremony. Your woman asked us to come be a part of this special day and it is an honor for us to share in this time. Have you spoken to your holy man yet?"

"No," answered Reuben as he pointed at the approaching wagon train. "He is with those wagons."

Little Raven looked at the white topped caravan, shaking his head. "And still they come," and looking back to Reuben, he added, "My warriors will prepare the sweat lodge for you. You must cleanse yourself before you do this thing. Your holy man may join us if he wants, but you must do this."

Reuben cocked his head to the side, looking at the chief. "I will do this, but first I must find the pastor and speak with him."

"Good. We will put the lodge where the creek joins the river. It will be ready soon," explained Little Raven as he turned away to oversee the warriors at work.

"But aren't they Mormon?" asked the pastor after Reuben explained himself.

"Yes, but that was a recent decision by her father and the women hadn't fully accepted the faith. I think it was as much a choice to have someone to travel with as anything. But Elly holds to the Christian faith as she learned it at their home church. She has accepted Christ as her savior and knows she's bound for Heaven and wanted to be certain I believed the same, which I do. That's why we want you to perform the ceremony, Pastor."

"I will be happy to, Reuben. But you also said the

Arapaho were..." he frowned as he spoke, wondering just how complicated things would become.

Reuben grinned. "Yeah, I just found out about that a few moments ago, but Elly is the one that invited them to be a part. However, Chief Little Raven said all they would do is help us prepare for the ceremony, but you would do the vows and such."

The pastor nodded, smiling. "Well, it'll be a first for me, but whatever you and your woman want is fine with me."

WORD SPREAD QUICKLY AMONG BOTH WAGON TRAINS, prompting the new arrivals to circle up and make camp in anticipation of a grand party, which everyone was excited about. The trip had been tiresome and there had been few times of gaiety and it would be a pleasant break from the dreary routine. Throughout the camps could be heard fiddles tuning, squeeze boxes moaning, jewsharps twanging, and mouth harps playing. People were hustling about, preparing foodstuffs and arranging clothing and more. The level of excitement continued to rise as the time neared.

The women with Red Bear had erected a teepee in a copse near the river and had brought Elly and her mother and sister into the lodge with them. They would prepare the bride to be for the coming time. Part of those preparations would be counsel from Red Bear and Abigail about the ways of a man and a woman, and the responsibilities of the wife. The two younger women and Elly's sister, Phoebe, would prepare the garments and the bride's hair. The site chosen for the ceremony was on a grassy flat in the shade of the tall cottonwoods near the river, the teepee close by and the sweat lodge removed a little way upstream.

The men with Little Raven had erected a sweat lodge, a small dome shaped brush hut, covered with blankets and hides, with a small entrance covered by a hanging blanket. Inside, a fire blazed on a bed of rocks while nearby sat two birchbark basins with water. The grassy flat was perfectly suited for the purpose.

Little Raven welcomed Reuben, motioning him to the side of the sweat lodge and began explaining, "You and I will go into the lodge while the men go to prepare the big fire for the celebration. You will disrobe," and motioning to a bundle that sat on a blanket beside the lodge, "and after the lodge, you will bathe in the stream, then put on the new clothes."

"That's it? Just a sweat bath and new clothes?" asked Reuben, suspecting more.

Little Raven grinned. "I will give you counsel while we are in there," nodding to the lodge. "The people will come soon, you must prepare," directed the chief, starting to remove his own tunic. Reuben followed suit and the two men crawled into the lodge, sitting opposite one another. The fire had burnt out, leaving hot coals on the hot rocks and with a nod to Reuben, Little Raven used a gourd to scoop up some water and splash it on the rocks. Steam exploded and filled the small lodge, covering the men and bringing the sweat. This was repeated several times as the men sweltered in the heat and moisture. All the while, Little Raven, spoke of the responsibilities of a man to his woman. "You will always provide for her and your family, even before yourself. You will protect her, be honest in all you do, not just with her, but with all others. As a man, you have the responsibility to lead, teach, cover your family with your life. If you fail in this, you fail as a man." He continued his counsel to include every aspect of marital life and his responsibilities as a part of whatever village he chose.

They soon left the lodge, diving into the cold clear water of the nearby creek and scrubbing themselves. But when they returned to the blanket beside the lodge, Reuben was surprised when the chief handed him the bundle and he opened it to find a new set of pale gold and beautifully beaded fringed buckskins. He looked to Little Raven with a question on his face and the chief smiled. "The women," and gave no other explanation.

The people from the wagons had already started to gather when Reuben and Little Raven came from the smaller clearing. He was surprised to see that someone had erected an arbor and covered it with a combination of prairie rose and blue violets and other greenery. The pastor stood alone on the far side of the arbor; his bible cradled in his arm at his side. The many people were gathered in groups, some intermingling with those of the other train. Several of the women, always the more friendly, were getting acquainted with others and some were busy at the crudely fashioned tabletops made from barrels and planks and covered with dishes and baskets of food. To the side of the table, the various musicians were tuning and getting acquainted. Reuben shook his head at all the hullabaloo that was occurring because he and Elly were getting wed.

He walked beside Little Raven who had donned a different tunic and wore his hair-pipe bone breastplate and put three feathers in his topknot. His long hair hung loosely over his shoulders and his entire countenance showed his stature among his people and the respect of those nearby. He was an impressive figure and stood a bit taller than Reuben but was broader of shoulder and deeper of chest.

Yet most were looking at Reuben in his new buckskins. The beadwork was intricate but not gaudy as it accented the yoke of the tunic, front and back. Fringe hung from the sleeves and britches; tufts of orange dyed rabbit fur dangling from the ends of the fringe. His high-topped moccasins had the toes beaded to match the tunic, and his hair was brushed back from his clean-shaven face.

The two men strode confidently to the arbor, their eyes on the pastor, but a collective gasp from the crowd turned their attention toward the teepee as the women emerged and stood to the side as Elly came from the lodge. She wore a white buckskin dress, fringed at the hem with the same orange dyed rabbit fur tufts attached. The yoke at her breasts was covered with an intricate design of a rising sun formed in beads. The ivory elk's teeth dangled beside tiny bells below the yoke but above the fringe that danced across her chest with every step. The long fringe at the edge of the sleeves was accented with the same-colored beads and tufts of rabbit fur. A beaded and matching headband held her golden locks away from her face and accented her rosy and dimpled cheeks. Her high-topped moccasins matched the dress and she walked with a confidence and grace that exemplified her beauty. Her broad smile and focused gaze were centered on Reuben as she neared the arbor and stood beside him.

Reuben was breathless, felt weak at the knees, but steadied himself as he heard Little Raven chuckle and whisper, "Breathe."

The pastor began, "Dearly beloved, we are gathered together to join this man and this woman in holy matrimony. A vow and commitment that is for the rest of their life. As we stand before our God, known as *Chebbeniathan* to our Arapaho friends and as God the father, our creator, we join Reuben and Elly in this commitment." He continued with the rest of the vows, speaking of their loyalty to one another and to their God and more, Reuben thought it was taking forever, but in truth was but a few short moments.

They joined hands and the pastor had them recite the vows to one another, then added, "Do you, Reuben Grundy, take this woman, Eleanor Ann McGuire, to be your lawfully wedded wife?" to which Reuben gladly responded, "I do," and continued to Elly with a similar vow. Once finished, he pronounced, "I now declare you to be husband and wife. You may now kiss the bride!" Reuben grinned and pulled a smiling Elly close, then bent to kiss her to which she gladly responded. When they pulled apart, the crowd erupted in cheers and shouts and the fiddles started playing.

The feasting and dancing continued into the beginning hours of dusk and the crowd began to disperse to their wagons and Elly's parents and Little Raven and his woman, Red Bear, came to the side of the newlyweds. Little Raven spoke, "You will go to your lodge. It is customary for the new couple to stay in the lodge for at least a week. My people will come for the lodge at that time."

"Little Raven, you have honored us with your presence, guidance and help. I can never thank you enough," stated Reuben, clasping the man's forearm, and cupping his shoulder in his hand.

Little Raven looked at the young man, grinned. "It is good to make new friends and you are a good man. My people have called your woman Meadowlark, and you as the Man with the Blue Horse. You are a friend to the Arapaho. Perhaps our trails will cross again."

"I hope so, Little Raven, I surely do."

Elly was hugging the women of the Arapaho, thanking them as they readied to leave. It would be dark when they returned to their village, but it promised to be a clear night and the moon was about half and would offer ample light for the way. The newlyweds and Elly's family waved as the small band departed. As they rode away, Elly drew close to Reuben, her arm around his waist, his over her shoulder, and they looked to her family.

"We'll be leaving in the morning, probably before you two are even awake," chuckled her father, "so we'll say our goodbyes now."

There were tight hugs, many tears, and many words left unsaid as the family parted and Reuben and Elly stood watching as they walked back to the wagons. She lifted her eyes to Reuben. "My husband, I am so happy. This has been a wonderful day, don't you think?"

"Of course, I do, and I am happy too. We've got our entire lives before us, and the stars are shinin' down on us and I believe God has blessed us." He smiled down on her, scooped her up in his arms and carried her into the marriage lodge, laughing and giggling all the way.

**BEST-SELLING AUTHOR B.N. RUNDELL TAKES YOU ON
A FAST-RIDE IN A WESTERN CLASSIC LIKE YOU'VE
NEVER SEEN BEFORE.**

It was new country, beautiful and wild and full of challenges.

When Reuben chose to start the new chapter of his life with a
partner, he had no inclination as to the trials that would come.
The sight of a war party of Cheyenne Dog soldiers caught their
attention when they saw two captive white women, and Elly's
insistence that they free them was the beginning of those
challenges. A confrontation with four bandits that wanted the
women presented another challenge, but when a federal
Marshall and the owner of the Overland Stage line challenge
Reuben with the task of securing a gold shipment from the gold
fields of Colorado and get it to the Union forces while Rebel
recruits want it for the Confederacy, raises the stakes in his
new role. Add in an attack by outlaws teamed up with renegade
Arapaho and Cheyenne, some desperado prospectors, and a
handful of confederate deserters, Reuben and Elly have their
work cut out for them...

But when they think they've got it handled, two orphaned
urchins tug at their heartstrings and complicate matters even
further.

AVAILABLE JANUARY 2022

Born and raised in Colorado into a family of ranchers and cowboys, **B.N. Rundell** is the youngest of seven sons. Juggling bull riding, skiing, and high school, graduation was a launching pad for a hitch in the Army Paratroopers. After the army, he finished his college education in Springfield, MO, and together with his wife and growing family, entered the ministry as a Baptist preacher.

Together, B.N. and Dawn raised four girls that are now married and have made them proud grandparents. With many years as a successful pastor and educator, he retired from the ministry and followed in the footsteps of his entrepreneurial father and started a successful insurance agency, which is now in the hands of his trusted nephew. He has also been a successful audiobook narrator and has recorded many books for several award-winning authors. Now finally realizing his life-long dream, B.N. has turned his efforts to writing a variety of books, from children's picture books and young adult adventure books, to the historical fiction and western genres which are his first love.

Printed in Great Britain
by Amazon

17188667R00144